Margot Hammond
2/2005

Eight Days in Provence

Note - I have changed some names for reasons of privacy, but the story is the truth of our eight days together. JH

Cover photograph, Michael Fairchild
Photographs, Jennifer Huntley

Rosalie Ink Publications ▪ PO Box 291 ▪ Cold Spring Harbor, NY 11724 ▪ RosalieInk.com
First Edition November 2004 ▪
Editing & Production by Terry Walton ▪ Design by Inger Gibb
Printed in the United States of America
Library of Congress Control Number: 2004096280 ▪ ISBN 0-9711869-1-X

*In fishing there is term called "catch and release."
The fisherman is there for the challenge, to stand in the roaring
stream, and for a moment be part of it. If he is lucky
the rainbow trout will be hooked by such a fisherman. His hook
will be barbless and it will hurt only a little when he
pulls it out. He will hold the fish in his hand, admiring its
colors, and then he will set it free.*

"I am convinced that I shall set my individuality free simply by staying here."

-Vincent van Gogh

For eight days in Provence I was truly happy. I knew that moments of joy and renewed possibility were to be recognized and savored. Usually they lasted only minutes, even seconds – the time it takes the wind to blow a crimson leaf from its branch. For much of my life they had passed unheralded. I ignored them, or when cloaked in the fog of depression, I resented their absence. Once, I was left shattered by betrayal, but when I put the pieces back together the world looked different. I could see blue sky through the glass, cracks and all. And so, as the soft sunlight in southern France had warmed the paintbrushes of artists before me, it began on that very first day to work its wonder on the deepest part of my soul.

I almost missed the train to Avignon.

"Go now, Madame. You must go now," the frantic woman behind the desk at the Hotel Deux Continents shouted at me. "There is a rail strike today. They are running only one train to Avignon."

Thirty minutes later I dragged my suitcase out of a taxi at Gare de Lyon. I expected to find panic and chaos at the station, but instead, people moved about as if nothing were different. Strikes are not unusual in Paris. Still, I did not relax until nestled in my assigned seat on the silver TGV bullet train, making its high-speed journey south.

At Avignon a small group stood next to a pile of multicolored backpacks and suitcases. These strangers would be my companions for the next eight days. A handsome young couple wearing matching tee shirts introduced themselves as our fearless guides, Annie and James. She was slender, brown haired, and when she smiled dimples creased her cheeks. He was angular in face and body, mischievous behind a rich brown mustache that covered the corners of his mouth. They were clearly at ease with each other.

Annie and James hurried us out of the station and into a white van and soon we were speeding along a nondescript highway. Annie pointed in the direction of the horizon. "Those are the Dentelles de Montmirail," she said. Her French accent was subtle, elegant. In the distance, white jagged rocks protruded like an every-which-way snow fence along a mound of dark green hills. Annie said it reminded her of a lace cap framing a young girl's face. "We'll be hiking very close to them tomorrow," she said.

An hour later we arrived at Vaison-la-Romaine, touted in guidebooks as "the Pompeii of France." It would be the first of many towns we visited famous for their Roman ruins. The van stopped on the edge of the road, close to a solid ochre-colored rock cliff, halfway up the hill to the medieval-era *Haute Ville*. The rest of the way was on foot.

The Hotel Beffroi stood at the end of a narrow cobblestone alley. Despite being sandwiched between decaying houses, the sixteenth century building felt more like the sprawling home of a French Comtesse. My room was on the second floor in a separate yet interconnected building. Upstairs, I took off my shoes and walked across the cool tile floor to push open the heavy shutters. Light slanted in, gentle and welcoming. Across the alley a wild garden clung to the hill and red climbing roses cascaded over the high wall. The room with its tall white stucco walls, the honey-colored armoire, the colors and layers of patterns on fabrics, was homey and very French. I felt as if I were spending the night in the Pierre Deux shop on Madison Avenue.

From the landing on the stairs I had seen a small pool in a garden. Just what I needed, I thought, a baptism of sorts, a way to immerse myself in this place, in this moment. Unpacking could wait. So could my normal urge to hit the ground running, exploring the sights. I changed into my bathing suit and went straight down to the pebbled terrace below.

The stones were warm beneath my feet. It was so quiet I felt like a trespasser, as I walked to the edge of the cliff and looked down on the Ouveze River. The water was low, exposing gray rocks along the shore. The red-roofed houses clinging to the river edge were safe now, but several years before, I learned, a flood had nearly swept Vaison-la-Romaine down to the sea. I walked back to the never treacherous pool and stepped into the cool water. I did not hesitate, but surrendered to its restorative powers. The warm water took my body away as I floated there, effortlessly. I looked at the sky and wondered when my thoughts and feelings would become part of this place too.

Afterwards, lying in the sun on red and orange patterned cushions, I heard James call to me. He was standing at a third floor window. He filled the entire frame, as if he were standing on the windowsill. For a second I wondered how long he had been there. At the train station he had greeted me with, "And you must be Jenny." No one ever called me that. Even as a child I never used Jenny as a nickname. My mother always told me it sounded like a cow chewing on her cud. Jenny. But when James had said it, with his soft Australian accent, it sounded so familiar. For a moment I thought, maybe on this trip I will be someone different; I will be Jenny the way James said it. But out of habit I had gently corrected him, repeating, "Jennifer."

When James joined me at the pool he was wearing a blue tank bathing suit, not the clumsy body-camouflaging shorts favored by American men. We talked easily, two strangers, mostly about our travels, impersonal things. He sat on a chaise across from me. The strong afternoon sun was behind him and every once in a while I had to shield my eyes from its intensity.

When we gathered for dinner in the small formal dining room of the main house, Annie announced that two members of our group were missing. A couple from Indiana, Peg and Tim, had flown in to Paris mid-morning and fallen victim to the rail strike. "I hope they will be here by midnight," Annie said. Ah, there but for the grace of God, I thought, and crossed my fingers, hoping my lucky star would stay with me for the rest of the trip.

Our group was small and in May we had the advantage of warm weather without the crowds that overtake Provence during the summer months. This had proved a successful way for me to travel on my own.

It was my father who passed on his wanderlust to me. During my marriage I forced my reluctant husband to endure trips to far off locations requiring immunizations for dangerous diseases. He usually got sick anyway. Ice cubes in Ecuador, a "thousand-year-old-egg" in Hong Kong, mosquitoes in Kenya; he fell victim to them all. I'd played nurse and then snuck off to see the sites alone, grateful for the iron-clad constitution handed down to me along with the wish for adventure in travel. Our marriage also fell victim to our many differences, as it happened, and too many years of sadness had nearly suffocated my joy in the discovery of new places.

But after the divorce, travel became the aloe for my wounds. I knew wandering the streets of Paris alone would make me feel vulnerable and lonely, so I sought the safe company of strangers. Joining a group of other hikers I could have companions during the day and for meals and my solitude when I wanted it. Others could field questions like where are we were going next, or why aren't the binoculars in the daypack and where are the extra socks?

That first evening in Provence, two other men at the table were also traveling solo and may have shared my sentiments. Charlie looked like a man enjoying retirement. He was tan and relaxed, perhaps because he had spent the previous week biking through the Loire valley. His hair was thinning, turning from gray to white, and I guessed he was in his late sixties. John was younger and small in stature with wavy sandy-brown hair, and shy or nervous or both. I would come to recognize his gentle qualities. Another John and his wife Sue were the casual, outdoorsy couple from Arizona. I felt no immediate rush to get to know them. That's what the trail was for.

When I returned to my room the fatigue of travel, trains, taxis and vans finally caught up with me. In the big empty bed I pulled the down comforter high up around my ears, closed my eyes and hoped I would sleep through the night.

But as often for me at the beginning of a trip, sleep was elusive. Caught as I was in a purgatory between conventional life and the promise of adventure, my thoughts fell prey to fear. It was not my choice to be a solo traveler. I had six years of practice, paying the "single supplement" charge as if it were a fine for a traffic ticket.

I had practice battling this ache in the darkness, this need for subduing the doubts. What was I running from? Or to? And why did I have to do it alone? Big beds in beautiful hotels were meant to be shared.

As if a white knight appearing on a distant hilltop, the glory of crimson roses climbing beneath my window returned to my memory. Comfort came from these thoughts and the softness of the feather pillow. I had come to France seeking peace from the warmth of the sun, expecting only nature's beauty. I would save my tears.

Perfect blue sky greeted our small group of traveling and walking strangers, the next morning. Annie waved her hand and we followed her down the rough cobblestones to the main road. Her long legs were tan and she bounced along as if she could go forever. A cotton scarf, a triangle of blue, held her long brown hair in place and she looked as if she belonged in this landscape. The rest of us trudged behind her in baseball caps and new tee shirts. Little John, as the younger of the two would come to be known, leaned forward against the incline of the road, thumbs tucked into the straps of his pack, which seemed awfully full for a short half-day hike. He also carried a waist pack. Tim and Peg looked weary but willing after their travel ordeal. They had arrived by taxi sometime during the night.

We spread out on the empty road, walking two or three abreast. This was farmland and each house we passed had a garden or small orchard. When I glanced behind me, back to a solitary hill above Vaison-la-Romaine, I saw the remains of a castle's square tower. It rose out of the solid rock, like a lighthouse keeping watch over all below.

Annie waited ahead next to a fence post, directing us onto a grassy footpath at the edge of a small vineyard. New tendrils sprouted from gnarled old trunks growing out of the dry, rocky soil. At the end of each row roses were beginning to bloom. The rose was a monitor of pests and disease in the vineyard, Annie told us. It withered first while the farmer had time to protect the precious grapes. The vineyard ended at the base of the forested hills and we turned onto a trail shaded by low open pines. Annie pointed to the ground where the earth had been disturbed, the dry leaves pushed aside. "A good sign for hunters

– wild boar have been here," she said. I looked through the trees up and down the hillside and shared an expression of concern with Peg and Sue.

We continued the gentle climb through the foothills of the Dentelles until we reached Séguret. The village was almost too pretty – narrow winding streets, pastel colored shutters and overflowing window boxes. Vaulted passageways led to quiet corners and we stopped to admire a fountain where water trickled from the mouths of terra cotta faces into plastic buckets filled with laundry.

At the end of town, under a covered watering trough, James was waiting with an elaborate picnic of salads, cheese and breads. He looked as if he had just stepped from the pages of the travel brochure, wearing a long, dark green apron over his khaki shorts. He had been born and raised in Australia and trained in Europe as a chef, he told me. Being a chef enabled him to travel almost anywhere in the world and find work, regardless of alien employment laws.

"Everyone needs to eat," he now said, and I saw the twinkle in his eye for the first time. "Once I prepared a meal for the Prime Minister of Austria," James continued, standing over me, watching me as I ate. "He must have liked it because he sent a handwritten note to me in the kitchen expressing his 'compliments to the chef.'" I wasn't sure whether James was trying to

"In the fullness of artistic life there is, and remains, and will always come back at times, that homesick longing for the truly ideal life that can never come true."

-Vincent van Gogh

impress me, or just enjoyed patting himself on the back.

"Did you try some of the local wine?" James had filled a large wooden barrel with ice and pulled out a narrow bottle. "The rosé here is extremely nice."

"If I have that, I'll never make it back to the hotel," I said.

"Oh, come on. You're on vacation," James said.

I tasted the pink wine. It was cool and crisp, nothing like the sugary rosé wine my friends and I drank when we were in college.

Smiling, I raised my glass to James. He nodded, accepting my compliment to the chef, and returned to the table to rearrange tomato slices topped with black olive tapenade. He was like a proud artist back at his canvas to correct a brush stroke. It was almost a shame to destroy his creation by eating it.

The men sat on a long wooden bench, resting their backs against the stone wall after savoring lunch and its wine, legs stretched out in front and crossed at the ankles. Charlie pulled his cap down over his eyes, and John's hands rested atop his stomach. Sated and content, we could have stayed there all afternoon.

Later as we left Séguret for the return to Hotel Beffroi, I stopped in front of a clump of slender blue irises, nestling beneath a cypress tree, framing the foreground of the view across the valley. Instantly I knew I had seen this image before and remembered the cypress trees painted by Van Gogh. The memory of pictures in art books and the scene before me superimposed themselves in my mind, the detail of reality giving way to the dancing brush strokes of color. My feet felt planted in that spot and tears tried to push their way forth from the backs of my eyes. I wanted to show someone what I saw, but I was alone. All I could do was reach for my camera and snap a photograph before rushing down the path to join the group.

That evening I arrived for dinner wearing the New York uniform: anything black. The silky tee shirt and matching long pants made me look slim and tall. A deliberate choice for this night. James directed me through the archway to the salon and I thought I felt his arm reach for my shoulder, but his hand never lit there and so I assumed I must have imagined it. Awaiting aperitifs in the living room, James pulled his chair next to mine. "I like this fabric," he said as he touched my knee.

Someone suggested a short walk to see the ruins of the Vaison castle before dinner. James told us the Counts of Toulouse built their *château* in the twelfth century on the highest point of the old town. They were true masters of their domain, controlling everyone and everything for as far as they could see.

Stepping out the door onto the uneven stones, James stayed to make sure I didn't fall. "Here, Jenny, take my arm." I slid my hand between his body and arm, gently feeling the muscle just above the bend in his elbow. And then I did something I could not remember having done before. I was not a flirt. Flirting was for silly girls or for those older women who didn't know how to carry their age gracefully. I had been raised in the preppy pink and green world of the North Shore of Long Island, where propriety meant wearing a skirt to Sunday lunch at my grandparents' house.

And yet, when James offered his arm I took it, and gave him just the slightest squeeze. It was a hint of an embrace, as if I were saying, "Yes, I can be playful or maybe anything else you might imagine. I can be your kind of Jenny." And then just as quickly I let go, leaving him to wonder.

Each morning in Provence thus far had been sunny, but the next day as we drove to the trailhead there was a mist in the air and we could see low clouds hanging over the hills beneath Mont Ventoux. Cézanne often painted this mountain. Depending on the light, he made it either blue or lavender, or sometimes a shimmering white. I had studied his landscapes in school – never imagining I would someday set foot on those same hills, or follow a trail to the top of that famous skyward triangle.

From the parking lot we joined the GR 4 trail, part of France's Grand Randonée network of walking paths. John and Sue were dressed like experienced mountain climbers. They had lots of gear. John showed off his strong legs in his trim khaki shorts and knee socks. Sue's blond hair was tucked up beneath a visor. Both carried collapsible hiking poles and sprinted ahead with ease while the rest of us followed behind James.

The path climbed gradually through alpine forests and occasional limestone shale fields. In the shade, the last remains of winter snows clung to jutting gray rocks. The trail itself bisected a rockslide and, as if crossing a tightrope, each of us inched our way single file across the slippery scree.

Once back in the trees we stopped for a break on an outcrop of large time-rounded boulders. James stood at the edge of the precipice and pointed in the direction of the green valley below. He looked like a teacher giving an outdoor lecture. I noticed we were wearing matching rolled blue bandanas around our necks.

The views to the valleys below reminded me of the Alps and the exhilaration I had once felt there. I had only recently discovered hiking. But as a young girl I had spent much of my time alone, escaping to the quiet woods behind our house. Hiking, walking on the trails, in forests and meadows, climbing mountains, scrambling rocks and streams had become a new source of inspiration and peace.

This walk up Mont Ventoux was tame compared with other expeditions and hiking trips I had experienced more recently, in remote areas. My first real hiking experience came only when I was forty-two. Newly single I had traded emotional pain for the challenge of an Outward Bound course in the high sierra of California. The fifty-five-pound pack strapped to my back became a metaphor for my everyday obstacles and fears. At the end of that summer I felt exhilarated and brave. In the following years I chased after those feelings, seeking out adventures in far-flung places. If there was an element of danger, so much the better. I didn't see it as reckless to paddle down Class V rapids on the Bio-Bio River in Chile, or trek across remote areas of Tibet. But now I was ready for slow walks and no surprises. I wanted to soak up some *joie de vivre* in sun-drenched France.

A wrong turn at a hillside marker had us headed downhill off course for about a mile. When James finally realized the error we were faced with retracing our steps uphill, practically doubling our time to the summit. As we turned around on the narrow trail, someone asked, "How much further before lunch?"

Our group was tired, sweating and hungry and James hesitated before he admitted he wasn't sure how far we needed to go. So much for the leisurely lunch in an alpine meadow anticipated by us all. There was no more friendly chatter on the trail, either. We slogged along in silence.

I overheard Peg ask Tim, "Are you doing OK, honey?" He had slowed down and I dropped back to walk with them. She told me he was scheduled for a hip replacement when they returned from this trip.

James tried to redeem himself by leading us along a shortcut just south of the actual summit of Mont Ventoux. A large rock field, which I might have admired earlier for its surreal beauty, was now just a complicated obstacle course. Annie was waiting for us with the van in front of the roadside restaurant.

"You should have been here two hours ago," she scolded James. "I was getting worried."

"I'm not sure where I went wrong. You know that fork in the trail before you reach the meadow?" James began.

Annie cut him off, "We will have hardly any time this afternoon at Châteauneuf-du-Pape."

There was an intimacy in her annoyance, the kind saved for husbands and wives and easily forgiven later. Wondering, not for the first time, if they were a couple, I wasn't sure if Annie was really angry or just enjoying giving James a hard time. I didn't care. I just wanted to eat.

Le Chalet Rayard was a rest stop on a wide bend in the road up the side of Mont Ventoux. The winding road is famous for its hairpin turns and is sometimes used in the Tour de France. On this day vintage sports cars were speeding toward the top, downshifting and roaring past the restaurant. We were so late that the only thing left on the lunch menu was the *plat du jour*, lamb and beans, but we were ravenous and devoured it all, grizzled lamb and mushy lima beans. There were as many cloves of garlic in the sauce as beans, killing the taste but not the bacteria. As we sat in the afternoon sun and savored the hot meal, we were unaware that before long we would pay dearly for the *plat du jour*.

It was late afternoon when we reached our next hotel in the village of Sauveterre. In French the word means "safe ground." The village was built high enough above the Rhône River to be safe from its devastating floods.

Our hotel was a large white stone mansion covered in ivy and long past its glory days. A classic white elephant, it sat at the very end of a curved pebble drive. In front of the elegant old house huge, beautiful specimen trees flanked the defiant remains of a rose garden. An eccentric couple had bought the mansion, James explained, restored it themselves and opened a hotel and restaurant. It was a work in progress. The crumbling exterior was still grand and elegant, reminiscent of its heritage. The owner Marie Thérèse had done the interior design herself. She enthusiastically redecorated the main rooms with yards of flocked red velvet fabric and contrasting silver Mylar wallpaper. I thought I must have come across the only woman in France with bad taste.

James told us they were especially proud of their newest addition to the grounds, a secluded pool. It was already six o'clock, and at first I was ready to go straight to bed rather than face one of those long French dinners. I decided a swim might revive me.

A small path through the tall evergreens led to the pool. It was completely private, surrounded by shrubbery and sheltering cypress, a fairyland. Only the top of a simple bell tower jutting up over the treetops reminded me I was still firmly in France. The setting was so serene, the water so blue. I felt I was stepping into that famous Chanel No.5 ad as I eased myself into the water.

It was embracing, the water, cool at first and then soothing as I swam in smooth strokes. When I climbed out of the pool, the breeze on my wet body was cool and I was happy to put on the terry cloth robe provided by the hotel. I was leaning back on a chaise when I heard James approaching along the path. Impulsively I loosened the belt, letting the robe fall open just as he came into view. He was here for a swim also.

"God, look at you sitting there. I wish I had my camera." I felt self-conscious about my display and was tempted to pull the robe across me, but instead Jenny held her pose. I was committed now, just like taking that first step out onto the stage. You either remembered your lines, or you had to ad-lib it.

James dived into the pool at the deep end. "Oh, it feels great!" he said as he surfaced. His eyes danced, as if with invitation.

"Yes, I know."

"You've been in already?" He sounded disappointed.

This was the only time we had been alone since that first day when he had sat with the sun behind him at Vaison-la-Romaine. I watched him now, standing in the pool, the water cutting him in half at his waist. I had to fight the desire to stay in the fading sun wrapped in my warm robe. I moved quickly so as not to appear hesitant, to him or to myself, and stepped into the water.

We swam toward each other and then floated apart. There was a repetition and a rhythm to our movements, like small waves reaching for the beach and then pulling back. As we swam in circles together, we talked about the day, about simple things. But what I would remember long after we'd left the pool was that rhythm, like a gentle undertow pulling me closer to him.

Shadows from the tall trees chased the last of the sun away. It was nearly seven o'clock. Like two schoolchildren who had stayed too long at the playground, we had to rush home for supper.

My room was on the third floor this time, reached by climbing a steep narrow staircase. The rooms on that floor had all been remodeled in "contemporary" decor. The color scheme was black and white and turquoise. But the single most absurd element in these rooms was the gel ceiling. It was like Jell-O encased in plastic. I was tall enough to reach up and touch it, but recoiled when it moved. There must have been a reason other than design for this bizarre contraption. I didn't want to think of what might be trapped behind my gel ceiling. The one redeeming feature in the room was the large window overlooking the pebble terrace and garden. I opened the shutters and breathed in the cool evening air, as if this air with the scent and softness of a new place were slowly changing me.

I dressed quickly, choosing a long black skirt and a silver metallic tee shirt to complement the Mylar wallpaper in the public rooms.

The dining room was surprisingly sedate, painted a soft peach color. But Marie Thérèse could not leave well enough alone and had scattered small bouquets of plastic flowers on any available surface. Robert, her husband and the chef, had prepared our four-course meal, beginning with a salad of snow peas. James was delighted. "Ah, '*mange tout*'," he said. "It's what the French call them." Literally translated, it meant "Eat all." It was such an innocent and obvious name, the kind a child might invent for this vegetable – no shelling, no picking out the peas, just pop it in your mouth and savor its sweetness.

Our dinner was long, with many bottles of wine, but as we left the dining room James said, "Would you like to take a walk?" He made it sound totally spontaneous, almost an afterthought, but our eyes had met several times across the table and I'd sensed he was planning to ask me.

I took a breath and in the same tone replied, "Oh, yes, I guess it would be nice to get some air."

We walked out onto the pebble terrace and down the crumbling masonry steps. There was something so easy about James, the way he laughed when he made fun of himself. His mustache curled slightly upward when he smiled. I had been looking at him and watching my footing on the dark driveway, so I was surprised when I realized we were already in the town.

The harsh light from a bar across the street glared like an intruder. We crossed the square and returned to the dark, following a tree-lined alley toward an old house. Dry leaves were scattered on the path and crunched under our feet. It felt strangely eerie, like Halloween. I wondered if I were moving away from the safe ground of Sauveterre.

We climbed the stairs to a courtyard in front of the house. Still the tour guide, James was friendly and yet remote. He never took my hand, never stopped in the shadows to kiss me as I was imagining he might. As I was picking my way across the damp lawn near the courtyard, my foot landed in a hole and I tripped. "I'm fine, I'm fine," I said, hoping he hadn't heard the sound of my skirt tearing as I went down.

Regaining my balance on the road, I walked with James following its curves up a hill to an old stone church. I stopped in the light of the street lamp, pretending to be Marlene Dietrich, but James missed the performance and continued around the corner up a small flight of stairs. I followed him as he disappeared into the blackness. I thought we might be in a small park, but it was too dark to tell.

At a metal railing he stopped and I stood next to him, looking at the lights far down in the valley. They sparkled; sprawling across the horizon, it all seemed like the suburbs of an American city. The contrast annoyed me, standing in what I now saw was a garden behind the ancient stone church complete with bell tower, looking out at the mass of yellow and pink lights in a valley that could just as easily be Phoenix, Arizona. We were silent awhile, leaning on the railing.

"The air feels so soft," I said.

"Yes, it's caressing us," he said, after a moment.

But instead of turning toward me, he turned and walked away, letting the words float, balanced by silence before and after.

When I looked over my shoulder I saw him sitting on a bench about five feet behind me. In the dark the bench had been invisible, blending with the trunks and the walls of the church itself. I felt awkward standing alone at the railing and looked back at the lights in the valley. It was my move.

I wondered if he had been here before. How many times has he played this scene with other women? Not wanting to be just another one, I stayed at the railing. At least I could make him wait. Pondering my strategy, I began to realize it was actually I who was waiting and went and sat down on the bench. Several seconds passed.

"Would you like me to rub your neck?" he asked. Checkmate. I tried to be casual. Sure, we'd been hiking all day and maybe I was a little sore, so if a friend or even the guide asked if he could rub my neck, was that so unusual? And yes, maybe the scene was too romantic and seductive to resist, sitting in the dark, with that warm night air caressing us, just as James had said. He moved his hand across my neck, rubbing it in a therapeutic way.

"Ah yes, that's the place," I said, relaxing when he kneaded the tense muscle under my right shoulder, "That's the tight place, the one that holds all the secrets."

I was relaxing now, feeling happy and free to be here with this man I barely knew. I closed my eyes. Maybe this was my chance to be more than just an observer in romantic France. When he leaned over and kissed my neck it seemed completely natural. I leaned back against him, savoring his lips on my skin, wondering what he would do next.

When I turned my head he touched my cheek and stopped me, whispering in my ear, "No, we can't kiss." For an instant I thought, Oh no, not another nut, but then he added, "We can't kiss yet. We can't kiss until we can't stand it any longer."

I felt a combination of passion and relief. At last, a man who knew what he was doing. I leaned my head back against his shoulder as he continued to kiss my neck and ran his hand down my arm and along my leg. He was again the guide and I knew my real adventure with James was just beginning.

We didn't kiss that night. When we said goodnight at the front door of the hotel, standing in the shadows, he told me, "We will go to bed to dream about what might be."

There would be no romantic dreams that night, however. The rancid lamb we ingested at lunch had been silently fermenting ever since. Throughout the hotel most of the hiking party would be dealing with the intestinal firestorm in their respective bathrooms for much of the night. When I arrived at breakfast the next morning, I was so queasy I avoided even looking at James.

We began our day's walk along the village roads, past small houses, until we reached a path surrounded by tall grass and large clumps of bushes – a welcome sight for a few of the walkers who were still feeling the effects of our food poisoning. James tried to assure us that this was not a common occurrence. "We won't be eating in that roadside restaurant again," he said.

"You mean this doesn't happen on every trip?" I teased.

"No!" he scoffed. "It's not as if we're in some third world country."

He was right. You expected this kind of ailment in Mexico or India, but not in a country whose greatest contribution to civilization is arguably its cuisine.

When we arrived in Avignon, the morning's hike blessedly complete, Annie was waiting.

"You're on your own for lunch," she said. "We'll meet back here at two for a tour of the Palais des Papes." She turned and walked toward the center of town with James following close behind her, no glance for me.

I smarted just for a moment and turned to Charlie, standing conveniently nearby. "Care to join me for lunch?"

I didn't want to follow James and Annie and suggested instead we avoid the touristy cafés of Avignon. Charlie followed me down a narrow passage alongside the palaces. He wore a faded plaid shirt and tan shorts and his manner was pleasant, a comfortable partner for these explorations.

We wandered along the constricted way. It was like walking through a tunnel blasted into solid rock. Walls seemed to grow right out of the limestone cliffs. We crossed under a flying buttress pushing against the wall of a newer building. Someone had painted the window frame a bright yellow – a cheerful touch just caught by the sun as we went by. I could almost reach out and touch both sides of this stone canyon. I felt as if we had discovered a secret passage once used by monks and Roman soldiers. Dusty green tufts of wild plants grew wherever soil collected in cracks. From somewhere beyond, I could hear languid notes of slow jazz from a lone saxophone.

The path soon converged with several streets and the one we chose became more commercial the further we walked. Dull looking shops selling newspapers, candy and art supplies behind dirty windows crowded the sidewalk. Without our guides we were heading away from the picturesque parts of Avignon. I gave up the idea of finding the perfect lunch place when we came to a large, anonymous gray square with two cafés. We picked one and ordered ordinary tuna sandwiches. Refreshing after yesterday's repast.

Charlie and I shared stories of our travels over lunch. He was the oldest person on this trip but one of the strongest walkers. He took many hiking trips, often on his own. He had a lady-friend and sometimes they traveled together, but she preferred less active vacations. I decided Charlie was a nice man and, apparently, a more dependable lunch date than James. Our time was relaxed, delightful in fact.

We arrived back at the Palais des Papes a little before two o'clock. People were gathering in the huge square. Teenagers sprawled across the wide steps leading upward to the Palais entrance. The sun was still high so cast no shadows on the courtyard of the looming Gothic palaces, rendering everything flat shades of beige. These medieval palaces were built in the fourteenth century, we learned from Annie, when the seat of the papacy was moved from Rome to Avignon. But the grandeur and wealth the popes had brought to Avignon disappeared slowly over the centuries, leaving the palaces bare, skeletal survivors of a once resplendent era. I felt guilty at my sudden attack of laziness and lack of interest in exploring this piece of history. An afternoon nap would have pleased me far more.

Obediently I followed our group inside. Annie bought the tickets while James scanned the crowd. He waved his arm and led us into an open courtyard, approaching a sandy-haired young man. Marco, our local guide, was from Holland and spoke English with such a heavy Dutch accent I had to strain to understand what he was saying. I found it hard to look at him for any length of time without giggling. He had bad skin and wore a single gold hoop earring with a dangling pearl. The pearl jiggled back and forth when he spoke. Marco recited his memorized guide speech as he led us through huge rooms with bare walls. The colorful frescoes and Flemish tapestries once adorning the walls were long gone.

In the banquet hall we stopped in front of the portraits of the ruling popes. I spread my feet apart, arms folded, and settled in for a long semi-coherent speech by Marco.

Our group was clustered together. James stopped for a moment behind me and then moved around the outside of the group as if trying to get a better view. He appeared to be concentrating on Marco's lecture as he slowly moved along the periphery of bodies, like a dog containing a herd of sheep. When he stopped moving he was so close to me I could almost feel the heat from his body, the jet stream of his breath moving behind me. He stayed for only a moment, just long enough for the heat, his warm breeze, to reach me, and then moved on.

Each time he circled and stopped next to me I felt momentarily paralyzed, as if a small electric current ran up my neck, leaving me woozy. I was sure he was doing this intentionally and I looked over at him and smiled, but he did not appear to notice. Could he really be so interested in Marco's monotone descriptions of the lifestyles of the rich and famous popes?

The pleasant buzz in my head stayed with me as we entered the papal bedroom. Maybe this was another one of James's games, a way to keep the tour interesting.

In the small room we gathered in front of the bed covered in blue and red fabric once rich but faded to soft colors now. The others stopped, but I continued moving, like a fish swimming upstream, until I was standing next to James. I pretended to study the dark blue walls covered with gold stars, dimmed but still bespeaking elegance. I tried to appear serious, staring at the wall.

"Let's continue to the next room," Marco said. I glanced at James and thought I saw a small knowing smile on his face. We continued this silent seductive dance throughout the remaining rooms, never quite making eye contact, pretending to be intent students of history. What if we lingered behind in one of the rooms, I wondered, maybe the Pope's bedroom? But I meekly followed the others down the steps into the Great Hall, the spell now broken. Outside we climbed to the top of a tower and looked out over the river. As I passed James on the way down mischief overcame me and I whispered, "Was it good for you?"

No visit to Avignon is complete without a walk on the bridge, the Pont d'Avignon immortalized in the French nursery rhyme we can all still hear in our heads. The four remaining arches of the stone bridge leapfrog across the glistening river, ending abruptly as if bombed during the war. But no. Since construction eight centuries ago, we learned, it was the ravages of the Rhône River that eventually got the better of the bridge. Floodwaters washed away each attempt to rebuild it, and eventually the townsfolk simply gave up, leaving a tourist attraction for modern day visitors.

"How does that song go?" Peg asked. "Oh, sing it."

Annie began to sing the children's nursery rhyme, " *Sur le pont, d'Avignon. . . .*"

"You sing too, James," Peg commanded. She made James and Annie pose repeatedly, dancing in circles singing, "*L'on y danse, l'on y danse . . .*"

When Peg cried, "Do it again," I turned and walked back to the town. Such is the life of a tour guide.

It was late afternoon when we returned to the hotel in Sauveterre. As I climbed the stairs to my garret room on the third floor I realized how hot and tired I was. I collapsed on my bed spread-eagled, enjoying the breeze from the open window. After the pseudo erotic trip through the Popes' palaces, I felt as if I should be smoking a cigarette.

The telephone rang, startling me. When traveling alone I want to feel like a solitary soul in a new land, in the present with no future and no past. I never phone home, and I do not want anyone calling me. A phone ringing in a foreign hotel room usually signals trouble.

I picked up the receiver and heard a deep voice with an Australian accent, "Hellooo . . . "

James continued, "What are you doing?"

Before I could answer he said, "Listen, would you like to join me for a drink before dinner?"

I felt that familiar excitement slowly rising inside me. Even in my mid-forties it felt the same, anticipation of adventure about to begin. It was a feeling full of hope and youth, like the first kiss from the red-haired boy on the beach by the big rock so long ago.

Time had worn away at my zestful innocence. Fatigue and the promise of a nap tempted me now. In a way, I was frustrated by this intrusion. For a few moments in my simple room there had been no James, no imminent tryst, no past or its memories; only a psychedelic orange gel ceiling. I could close my eyes and relax. Instead, I was saying, "Oh, sure! That would be nice."

"Would you like to come to my room, then?" he asked.

"No, I don't think so," I answered, playing at sounding coy.

"Alright," he laughed. "How about meeting me on the terrace?"

"Yes, that will be fine," I said, sounding very prim and proper. I was pleased I had actually said no to his suggestion for a meeting in his room. Oftentimes I had been a spineless pushover for charming men.

"Around seven o'clock okay?" he asked.

"Yes," I said.

"Alright, see you then."

I climbed off the bed and went into the bathroom to wash my hair.

The shower was warm, evocative, a smooth stream of water running down my back. Finding romance after eighteen years of being a conventional wife and mother was like restarting the pause button on a video tape player. In an impulsive moment two years after my divorce, I had sent a note to my college sweetheart. "Remember me?" I wrote. Twenty-three years evaporated in seconds and we spent another two years flying across the country for romantic, torrid reunions. But just like the first time it didn't last, and I felt the same aching disappointment.

Standing in front of the bathroom mirror carefully tracing black eyeliner across my eyelid, I longed to be cool and blasé when I met James on the terrace. My experience with romance had left me cautious, but I was becoming Jenny on this trip.

For my cocktail rendezvous with James, I put on a scoop-necked sleeveless dress that ended just above my ankles. It's the color of port wine, I thought, feeling as if I were falling under a spell. The days in the sun had tanned my arms and face, and lent reddish highlights to my dark brown hair. Even in my plain black sandals, I felt like Cinderella emerging from my garret room. The red carpet on its white marble staircase looked regal instead of moth-eaten, and I practically floated down in one seamless motion.

It was still light on the terrace. The heat from the stones rose to meet the cool air of an almost summer evening. It reminded me of the last days at boarding school, when classes were finished and vacation meant freedom.

I was the first to arrive, and chose a small white wrought-iron bench as my seat, just big enough for two. But I was afraid I looked like some Southern belle waiting for her gentleman caller, and moved quickly to a chair next to the round table nearby.

"I'm sorry I'm late," James said, coming onto the terrace. He sat in the chair across from me. He wore loose-fitting navy cotton pants, a button down blue jean shirt and a tie with a huge cartoon character snarling, ready to jump off the fabric and attack at any moment.

"Do you like my tie? It's a Tasmanian devil."

I looked at his face. His brown eyes were smiling at me, like those of a mischievous bad boy. I decided to ignore the Tasmanian devil.

James had something I wanted. He was lighthearted, an Aussie with that "no worries, mate" attitude. I remembered my friends always telling me, "You think too much." It was time to heed their counsel.

Robert, the proprietor, soon came through the door carrying a tray with two glasses and a small pitcher of water.

"I ordered us two Pastis. I hope that's okay. It's the local drink of Provence," James explained.

Robert poured the water into the glasses turning the yellow liquor a milky white. He looked at me and held my glance just a second too long as he was leaving, the way most Frenchmen do. As I took a first sip, I raised my leg slightly to place my foot on the near edge of James's chair.

"I had the strangest dream last night," I told him. "I was with this man. He had an unusual accent. We were in a park or something and I was leaning back against him. He was rubbing my neck. And when I turned to look at him, he told me we couldn't kiss."

"Really? And you thought that was strange?" He was laughing. The last of the sun made his tan seem rich, his face singled out as if just for my glances. James was one of those men who would always retain his boyish looks no matter his age. That youthful charm, the playful glint in his eyes, inoculated him from what might sound sleazy coming from the mouth of a French gigolo. I wondered if mothers of sons, as I am, were especially susceptible to this charisma.

"Well . . ." I lowered my eyes, disarmed, not knowing what to say next. "Is it time for dinner?"

When I start falling for a guy I stop eating. I can almost measure how hard I'm going to fall by the amount left on my plate. I was unaware of my lack of interest in our dinner until dessert arrived. A gooey confection, swirls of red and white and a puff of whipped cream, would usually be irresistible to me. I tasted it and abandoned my fork on the side of the plate. Charlie leaned over. His plate was empty. "Aren't you going to finish that?" he asked.

"No, please take it," I said.

"You ate hardly anything," Charlie said with bewilderment.

While others "oohed and ahhhed" I felt annoyed when the waiter brought out still more – the huge tray of cheeses for our last course. Chèvre with ashes, chèvre without ashes, chèvre that had fallen on the kitchen floor last week and was just discovered this morning under a dusty table, runny Brie, not-so-runny Brie, the selection seemed endless.

At last it was time to leave the dining room. As we walked through the doorway, James said, "I'll just run and get a sweater." I walked out onto the terrace where others had gathered at the edge of the stone wall. I had brought along my cashmere shawl and pulled it around my shoulders now, walking further to the right and finding myself on the darkened path to the pool.

The water itself was lit and the green glow illuminated the adjacent cypress trees. I stood quietly in the soft light, waiting, seeing yet another tall bell tower just beyond the garden boundary. The sky was black except for a pale haze around the peak of the tower. I wanted James to find me here, to ride in on his white horse. When he didn't appear I started back toward the house, but turned into a wooded area just before the bright lights of the terrace found me.

I heard the briefest sound and looked back. James was walking toward me. Neither of us spoke, but we continued to move nearer to each other. Two magnets silently drawn together. And even when we touched it seemed we did not stop the pull. He kissed me, softly at first and then stronger and harder, pulling me steadily to him. When we pulled apart he silently took my hand and we walked through the trees away from the hotel. When we were almost at the end of the drive, he looked at me like a co-conspirator, "I've gotten the back door key from Robert so we don't have to worry about being locked out."

As we came to the stone pillars at the entrance of the driveway, Little John appeared. Quickly James released my hand, as if he'd been caught shoplifting.

"Are you going for a walk in town?" he asked hopefully, falling in stride.

I crossed the small town square, now sandwiched between James and John, and I said, "It looks so different now." We followed the road up a hill behind the hotel and above the old church. We passed the little park and came to the entrance of a graveyard. There was no moon in the sky, but we could see the outline of white pathways and several large above-ground mausoleums. I climbed some steps and saw more tombs. It did not feel scary at all. I felt only excitement. Mischievously I turned and looked down at John and James, barely discernible in the shadows. Clutching my shawl in both hands I raised my arms to my sides. "Wooo," I laughed, swooping down the steps toward them.

"Look, it's the angel of darkness," James said.

We strolled back down to the hotel and casually said goodnight like three old friends. The lights were low in the silent lobby. I walked slowly up the stairs, letting John get ahead of us. We had almost reached the second floor landing when

James stopped. I was on the step behind him. He turned and whispered, "Come to my room. Five minutes."

I tiptoed down the dark hallway to my room. My hand fumbled in my pocket and silently I cursed the oversized room key as it clanged against the lock of my door. Inside, the brightness overhead blinded me. It was as if I had just stepped into police headquarters and some burly detectives were waiting to give me the third degree. I stood in front of the mirror. In the glare my reflection looked stark, like a mug shot. What should I do now? Slither back down the stairs to his room like a well-rehearsed lady of the evening? Or crawl into my bed and get a good night's sleep?

I looked away from the inquisitioned person in the mirror, threw my shawl on the bed and slipped out of my shoes. My hand reached for the door as I stepped into the dark hallway. In my bare feet I crept down the stairs.

I laughed at myself now, a grown woman "sneaking out." No opportunities had presented themselves to me as a young teenager. At my all-girls boarding school that kind of bravado would have meant expulsion. I obeyed the rules. But by senior year I'd spent almost four years nestled in this protective fold on a hill overlooking the Hudson River. That winter I was in a play with the neighboring boys' school and by spring the

English exchange-student who played the vicar was my boyfriend. One night I did break the rules.

Succumbing to spring fever, I walked off campus at dusk, down the village streets to the station, and met my "vicar" as he got off the train. We kissed on the hill overlooking the river, a passionate-innocent interlude of mere hours, until he caught the next train heading north. Back in my dorm room I acted as if I had just returned from the library, but my heart was pounding.

I felt the same bad-girl excitement now in the stillness of the quiet hotel.

The second floor landing was dark and empty. I had seen James turn to the right when I left to go up to my room. Long velvet drapes hung from the ceiling. They parted in the center. Beyond was the door to the bedroom, discreetly ajar. Light spilled onto the carpet from the bathroom at the far end of the room. I heard water running. My breath caught in my throat and I stepped back into the space between door and drapery. I had expected him to be waiting for me, maybe with a glass of wine, something romantic.

The heavy fabric smelled musty as I stood there trying to silence my breathing. Maybe this wasn't such a good idea, I thought, lingering in my dark Purgatory, somewhere between safe and boring and the hope for more. It's not too late to back out, I told myself, but then I heard his footsteps inside the room and felt my arm reach forward, pushing open the door.

The yellow glow from a lamp made everything in the room look even older than it was. An antique armoire sat against one wall. The carpet was a worn pattern of ochre and browns. Two tall windows stood open to the warm night air. James was dressed only in a white terry cloth bathrobe.

"That's a little presumptuous, don't you think?" I blurted out, pointing to the robe. I was embarrassed that he looked so ready for action.

"What do you mean?" he said. His eyes held the hint of laughter. I felt silly, irresolute. Then as if to reassure me, he playfully showed me his brightly colored silk shorts under the robe. "I can put some clothes on if you like."

I shook my head and laughed at myself. I was in his room, after all. The decision had been mine.

"Come here," he said, lowering his voice. He kissed me gently as he guided me to the bed and then, with practiced hand, pressed me down against the pillows. His lips were on my neck. My hands were in his hair. It was fine and soft like a baby's hair. He whispered to me in that lovely accent and I could hear my own voice saying his name. "James. James."

It sounded strangely familiar, but I wasn't sure why. I had never known anyone named James. Boys in America were called Jim or Jimmy. James sounded sophisticated and foreign.

I began to have an almost uncontrollable urge to say his name with a Russian accent. "James, Oh, James." The memory returned to me: a darkened theater, captivated by the man on the giant screen. It was my first time with him, the first time I heard his name. It came from her lips like a purr. "James." Rolling around on the sheets in Sauveterre, I'd become Tatiana Romanov with 007, James Bond in the movie *From Russia With Love*. I suppressed a giggle, losing the moment of passion.

"How old are you?" I asked.

"I'm thirty-nine."

Almost ten years, I thought to myself. "Do you know how old I am?" I asked, sounding like a little girl.

"Of course I do," he laughed, "I'm the guide, remember?"

Maybe it was because he was not American, maybe it was because we were in France where pleasures are meant to be savored, or maybe it was because he was a chef trained to taste one course at a time. Whatever the reason, we did not make love that night. He did not have that sense of urgency I had expected. I sensed he had a plan. And I decided he would be welcome as my guide here, as well as on the trail. . . .

Later, before I left his room, I went to the window and leaned over the edge, breathing in the night air. James came and stood behind me. His arms were wrapped around my waist, and his chin rested on my shoulder. The trees in the garden were lit from below. We stood there silently looking out at the darkness for a long while. I felt another defensive layer slip away. The wind caught the thin curtains and blew them back into the room. I turned and quietly walked to the door. "Good night," I said.

The sun shining through the shutters of my window awakened me before the alarm had a chance to ring. I had an unfamiliar feeling of serenity. My mind was strangely clear, uncluttered. As I dressed I realized I wasn't even sure where we were going that day and I did not care.

I walked down the long stairway to the lobby. Robert, last night's chef and keeper of the keys, stood behind the white marble front desk, watching my every step. Wearing a lecherous and all-knowing smile he inquired, "*Bonne nuit?*"

On the terrace we ate our breakfast of hard rolls and butter and lavender honey. I sat facing the front of the hotel, and watched as the young house girls opened the tall, weathered shutters, greeting the day. They spread their arms wide pushing the shutters back against the ivy-covered walls, as if they were doing the breaststroke. The sunlight on their young faces made their skin seem iridescent. Charmed now by the place, I

"We saw a red vineyard, all red like red wine. In the distance it turned to yellow, and then a green sky with the sun, the earth after the rain violet, sparkling yellow here and there where it caught the reflection of the setting sun."

-Vincent van Gogh

was sorry we were leaving Sauveterre.

After breakfast we packed, loaded the van and drove to the trailhead in La Garrigue, the rocky moors of Provence. Annie counted heads like a schoolteacher, as we stood knee deep in the scrubby, flowering bushes. "*Allez, les enfants!*" she called, heading down the path, which soon became a tunnel of green.

When Annie stopped to answer someone's question about flora and fauna I continued on, leaving the group behind. It was cool heading downhill. The silvery leaves of wild olive trees and a canopy of oaks shaded the trail. A sea of ivy lapped at my feet and small birds chirped overhead. It's what I loved, being alone in the forest.

I came to a place at the bottom of the hill where runoff from spring rains had deposited silt and beige pebbles as if at the mouth of a river. All was quiet in the sun with no sound of the hikers. I scrambled up a path to the left and perched myself on a large boulder overlooking the clearing below, and waited. Nearby on top of this hill, rectangular blocks of stone protruded over the edge. Later I would realize I was standing atop the ruins of a Roman aqueduct.

"Hey, I'm up here," I shouted as the group came into view. Without looking up, they drank from their water bottles and followed the trail into the woods. Had they heard me? I rushed down, vaguely disappointed, running to catch up. James was in the sweep position, bringing up the rear, making sure no one got lost. I fell in line in front of him, like the last of the little ducklings in a children's book.

Conversations on the trail are often conducted in short, simple sentences aimed at the back of someone's head. They pound out the rhythm of the steps, a diversion when the trail is tedious or a push when the going gets tough. And since hikers are rarely face-to-face, that anonymity sometimes leads to revealing conversations.

"So, do you have any children?" James asked me.

" One son," I answered over my shoulder. "He's sixteen."

"Really?" he said, sounding oddly surprised. "I have a son who is sixteen." He hesitated, "But I was never married. Do you find that shocking?"

"It does happen," I said.

"Actually I was really young at the time. I was just twenty-one, a boy really. She was older than I was," he hesitated for a moment, "and she was married. Well, her marriage was ending, but that kind of put it over the edge."

"Did you think about marrying her?" I asked.

"She didn't want to. She did eventually marry again and they have a daughter now. We all get along really well. You know, celebrating the holidays together," he laughed, "one big family." He continued, as if he couldn't stop now, his words escaping into the woods, not necessarily for me. "When she was trying to get pregnant with her new husband she said to me, 'Why can't I just have another baby with you, James? We make such beautiful babies.'"

I looked up and saw the group waiting for us on an asphalt road just ahead. The wooded trail ended before I had a chance to think about what James had just told me. We marched onward to the Pont du Gard.

Built by the Romans two thousand years ago as an aqueduct to bring fresh water to Nîmes from a spring near Uzès, Annie explained, the bridge still spans the Gard River. In this land with so many Roman ruins, I was amazed to see three levels of staggered half moon shapes intact, seemingly untouched by the centuries. Full trees and brush along the river's banks enveloped each end of the Pont du Gard, disguising the crumbling end of the span.

We climbed a steep dirt path to the top and walked part of the way across the bridge – another photo opportunity for all. I tried to sound nonchalant when I asked Annie to take a shot of me with James. It would be the only picture I would have of us together. We stood next to each other, casually, trying not to touch, merely guide and client. Later whenever I looked at that photograph I would see his arm pressed possessively against my side. He must have moved it just before the photo was snapped.

We drove to the town of Uzès for lunch. At an outdoor café in the town square, we sat at long tables in two rows under yellow and white umbrellas. We must have looked like small children at a birthday party, suspiciously surveying the plates of lettuce, strange cured meat and little boiled potatoes.

I took off my hiking boots and stretched my legs under the table. James sat across from me. When he began to talk to others at the table, I raised my leg slightly and began running my foot up and down his bare leg. He started to laugh, but quickly regained his composure. I looked away and joined in the conversation about some aspect of Pop American culture. As I spoke, I straightened my leg and allowed my foot to travel up his thigh. From the waist up I appeared calm as I coaxed the potatoes across a lettuce leaf. The prongs on my fork traced the white lines of fat in the sliced salami, while beneath the tablecloth my toes danced and teased.

When we left the table James smiled ever so slightly and looked down at my plate. "You hardly ate any of your lunch," he said.

The town was quiet in early afternoon, everyone enjoying the French version of a siesta. We walked down a narrow street, the light limestone walls of the houses made charming by their bright blue shutters. Above us, a third floor window slowly opened as a young woman leaned forward.

"I love to see the women opening the shutters," Annie said. "To me, it is a moment of *sensualité*."

On a hill far above the Gard River lay the hamlet of Castillon du Gard. We drove past the small, empty town square. In the mid-afternoon sun the village was bathed in a soft yellow light, highlighting the surrounding terra cotta tile roofs. A tiny gray-stone church cast its shadow over an old fountain in the square. It was as if the inhabitants, hidden away in their ancient houses, had fallen under a sleeping spell. Our van turned off the main square and stopped close to the buildings, their rough old walls shaded by the narrowness of the street. Stepping out we had to press our bodies against the walls as we inched past the van. James led us single file down an even narrower side street to our hotel, Le Vieux Castillon.

Once inside the intimate lobby James began to distribute room keys. "Let's see, the Browns are in room six, that's just up the stairs to the right. And Peg and Tim, you're in room three just off the garden." When he came to me he said, "Your room is a little hard to find. Why don't you follow me and I'll show you where it is."

We climbed three steps and then turned down a long hallway. Afternoon light poured in through windows facing a courtyard garden and made square patterns on the carpet. The hotel had been an elegant old home, James told me, a crumbling ruin that had been restored while still preserving the character of the place. The original stone walls had been left standing wherever possible, the interior bright with freshly painted pale walls and large urns of fresh flowers. This mixture of ancient and new was magical. I looked out the windows and saw flowering vines and lush shrubbery surrounding a tiny, bubbling fountain. At the end of the hall we stopped in front of an arched doorway.

"So, have you put me in a room as far away from the others as possible?" I asked.

"My room is just down those stairs," he said. "And I thought you'd like to be closer to the pool."

"Very thoughtful." I glanced at him over my shoulder, secretly pleased at the arrangements.

James turned the key and opened the door. I stepped inside a small living room. A lush, blue velvet couch made the room look elegant. It faced a single French door painted white and opening onto a red-tiled terrace. At the far end of the room a spiral staircase coiled upwards. "It's beautiful," I said softly, my voice conveying my pleasure.

"Look upstairs," James smiled, pleased with himself.

I climbed the circular stairs, stopping to look out a small

round window, like a porthole, to the street below. The room at the top was like an attic hideaway. The wood walls smelled of dry, warm afternoons in a pine forest. A huge bed dominated the room. I laughed out loud just as James appeared at the top of the stairs.

"What did you do, give me the best room in the house?" I asked. Then I added, "Thank you. This is really fabulous."

"Wait until you see the pool." He turned and disappeared, vanishing down the stairway. I almost expected to see a puff of smoke. I was left staring at the pattern of bright-petaled red flowers on the bedspread. I started down the staircase, but it was very narrow, like a tightly wound spring, and I had to move slowly so as not to slip. When I reached the first floor James was just leaving. "I'll see you at the pool," he said.

I opened my suitcase and rummaged through the clothes until I felt the smooth texture of my blue bathing suit. Undressing in the living room, I threw my clothes on the couch and slipped into the suit and pulled on a pair of khaki shorts. I went in search of the pool, retracing my steps down the long hallway. A door led to the small garden. Immediately the grandly overgrown vegetation enveloped me, making me feel insignificant. Flowers floated above large green leaves, and vines wove their way up the gritty stone walls as if answering a snake charmer's call. The pathway led around a small fountain and I climbed several steps to a large single story building. Tables inside were set with white linen.

To the right of the dining room wide, shallow steps led to an expansive terrace and, at last, the pool. It seemed to float above on the stone slab of the terrace – a long rectangular sheet of shimmering turquoise blue. There were the usual chaises with white-and-blue-striped cushions plump and inviting, in small groupings.

But what gave the setting its surreal and dreamlike quality was the backdrop to it all. Not the picturesque vineyards or the rolling hills, but the remains of the exterior wall of the original house. It had been left standing, as if defiantly resisting attempts at demolition, a portal between past and present. A large square once holding a window was now a grand, gaping peephole to the horizon. Five or six steps were all that remained of an original stone stairway, hanging suspended halfway up the wall, and leading nowhere. The furthest wall ended in a sloping rock avalanche that crumbled to the ground. I felt as if I had walked into a Salvador Dali painting.

I found a chaise closest to the old wall and lay on my back, my head turned toward the sun. It was half an hour before James arrived, followed by Annie in a slim, black maillot bathing suit trimmed in white. Her self-confidence was almost childlike. She sat on the edge of the chaise where James lay on his back, his head propped on his interlaced hands. They laughed and touched each other in a playful, familiar way. I felt like the third wheel and decided to go for a swim. James dived in the pool directly after me.

"Do you want to have a race?" he asked.

I looked at him, trying to decide if I could beat him.

"Okay."

Annie counted from the edge of the pool, "One, two, three." I pushed off as hard as I could and concentrated on pulling myself through the water in long, smooth strokes. I reached the other side just a second after James. "She won!" shouted Annie, as if it was important for me to beat James.

"No, I didn't," I confessed. "He won, just by a hair."

I didn't wait for my bathing suit to dry, but put on my shorts and left the pool. James followed me through the side door to the hotel. "Would you like to see my room?" he asked.

I followed him down a small staircase, pushing aside thoughts of where I might really be going. His doorway was indeed right below mine. The room was large, but plain, not elegant like my elaborate suite. It too had an oversized bed.

"Check out the bathroom," James said as he walked to the side of the bed. An arched doorway constructed of original stone blocks led to a large bathroom. I had to duck my head to look inside. The ceiling was smooth concave plaster, connecting a series of rough stone arches. It looked as if it had once been a tunnel leading to the dungeon of a Gothic castle. Now it was a huge marble bathroom, complete with Jacuzzi.

I was about to say something when I felt James's hand grab the back of my head. He yanked my hair hard and in one quick motion pulled me from the doorway and shoved me against the rough stone of the wall. He still held my hair as he kissed me, his other hand on the damp bathing suit that clung to me like a second skin. He had the same intensity I'd felt the night we first kissed in the woods at Sauveterre. My knees began to go soft and the grit from the stone dug into my back. He unbuttoned my shorts and they seemed instantly to fall to the floor. Only a few seconds had passed, but I felt suspended in time. Again in one motion he threw me onto the bed and was on top of me.

How can I explain what happened next? We come to expect certain patterns of behavior. Predictable patterns. Maybe that's why something that was once exciting becomes routine, boring. James had me pinned to the bed, helpless, each breath escaping like a gust of wind. He could have torn off my clothes and we could have made mad passionate love, as they say. But just when I thought I knew what would happen next, he stopped and raised himself up on both hands, and simply looked at me. He appeared to be pondering a question, trying to make a choice. One side of his mouth turned up slightly in the beginning of a smile, almost triumphant. And without his saying a word I read it all in his face. No, not now, not yet. And I knew he was right. "We can't . . . until we can't stand it any longer," he'd said in Sauveterre.

When I left his room I offered my best parting shot, "Nice bathroom," I said, as I closed the door.

That evening I dressed for dinner in black pants and black blouse, which made me look even taller than I am and more importantly, thin. The hotel's restaurant had received one star in the prestigious Michelin guide. Even one star in France is considered an incredible honor and assurance of a special meal.

We gathered for drinks in the small lounge, decorated with sleek, upholstered furniture in shades of pale green. Large glass windows overlooked the terrace as dusk stole the last sunlight of the day.

Annie walked in dressed all in white. Her hair was pulled back and she wore pearl earrings. She looked beautiful, and the men joined in a chorus of "Oohs" and "Wow" and "You look like an angel." I stood next to her and recited, "Once there were two sisters. One was very, very good, and one was very, very bad." We laughed and sat on either side of Charlie on the arms of his chair and called ourselves Charlie's angels.

James stood by the bar, holding a glass of champagne and smiling, like the host. He was dressed up for the evening, wearing long pants and a button-down shirt. This was his element. He loved fine food and wine and the camaraderie it engendered. Like a proud father, he watched as the waiter passed an hors d'oeuvre to each of us.

Small gold teaspoons were arranged in a circle on a silver tray filled with orange smoked salmon, a swirl of *crème fraiche* topped with several small black mounds of caviar and, finally, slivers of gold leaf. I took one and put the spoon in my mouth upside down as if I were eating ice cream. "It's called *amuse-bouche.* Something to whet the appetite." James's thick brown mustache turned up a bit as he smiled.

"An amusement for the mouth," I said, thinking out loud, literally translating the words to English. The gold leaf seemed almost too decadent, the kind of thing Marie Antoinette would have popped into her mouth before she said, "Let them eat cake." The tray came around again, but this time I smiled, "No, thank you. I've had my quota of heavy metals for the day," and sipped my champagne.

Our dinner was elegant. We sat at a round table covered in white linen, with many wine glasses. Waiters presented the main course on plates covered with silver domes. They stood behind our chairs until each entrée was in place. Then, in a magician's gesture, their white-gloved hands raised the domes in unison, revealing the delicate breast of a pigeon. In the candlelight everyone looked like my friend and I was happy to be in their company. We ate in comfortable leisure, and at the end of the meal waiters brought several plates of delicate sweets as beautiful as gems.

"These are also called *amuse-bouche*." James said.

"Ah, good," I said, our underground repartee continuing, "We all need more amusement."

One plate held a small round ball resembling a yellow cherry dusted with sugar. "That one is filled with cream and is called Cleopatra's nipple," he announced to the table. All male hands reached for it.

"Now wait," I cautioned, as if I were a teacher advising my class of the intricacies of food tasting. "The way to eat this is to first, close your eyes. Don't look. Just put it in your mouth and taste it." Someone taught me long ago, dulling one sense could intensify the others.

The women had reached for the chocolates. What started as a soft murmur grew into louder moans as ten people sat with eyes closed around the white table sharing the sensuous joy that can come only from dessert.

We were giddy after such a theatrical meal, spilling outside in the warm night air. The terrace was now lit and the glowing green pool and the floating staircase on the crumbling wall became our stage. Someone hoisted me onto the stairs and I tried to pose seductively while James snapped pictures. In front of the others I began to feel foolish, to feel exposed and vulnerable, and jumped from the bottom step.

We all walked further, strolling together through the deserted streets of the town. Beyond a low wall the glow of lights rose against the black landscape. Over the top of the wall I could see across darkened hills to the glorious, illuminated Pont du Gard.

After saying goodnight to all in the lobby, I followed James down the long hallway to our rooms. When we reached my door, he took my hand and led me silently down the stairs. We did not speak until we lay in each other's arms.

"Do you want to make love?" he asked, as if the question had just entered his mind, as if everything that had gone before were not some kind of calculated foreplay. Perhaps he needed me to give my permission. Or maybe he just wanted to hear me whisper, "Yes."

I don't remember what hour I left his room. I only remember hearing him say,

"Please stay."

The next morning, as we sped along the narrow country roads toward the Gorge du Gardon, the night at Castillon still savored, I looked out the window. James drove the van while Annie sat next to him discussing directions, laughing, excluding their passengers. She liked to tease him and when she did she called him James-ey.

"Remember that old lady in that funny guest house in Sault, James-ey? She liked you. Remember? She gave you a special large plate of gizzards." Annie was in a good mood. "What will you make us for lunch, James-ey?"

Peg and Tim sat with Charlie in the back seat, discussing the splendor of last night's meal. We drove through farmlands where the fields were bright green and lush. Spring's tender new crop had taken hold of the soil. Red poppies, iridescent and translucent in morning sun, slashed across the fields every now and then. They were shocking in their intensity, like a bleeding knife-wound to the green flesh. Rows of poplars, their black trunks perfectly aligned, separated road from field. Speeding by, the trunks looked like jailhouse bars. I wanted to break free, to run into the poppies, to smear the flowers on my skin in some ritual act, the way hunters smear the blood of their first kill. I wanted to swim through them, to sink down and be swallowed by red.

"Look at those poppies!" I said, wondering if anyone else even saw them.

"Ah, yes, they are like . . . a moment of *sensualité*," someone added, attempting a French accent, trying to sound like Annie.

"More like a moment of passion," I replied.

"You know, poppies are said to appear wherever the soil has been disturbed," James said. "You see them all across the battlefields in northern France. They say, wherever a soldier has fallen, poppies grow."

"That's why they're the symbol of veterans," I said, remembering from childhood the gray haired men in blue uniforms, selling small crepe paper poppies at parades.

We continued to pass farms and fields and each time we saw a flash of red I was afraid it would be the last. Finally I couldn't stand it any longer.

"Stop!" I cried.

Annie looked over her shoulder with concern.

"I have to take a picture of these poppies."

The flowers were taller than they'd seemed from the car window. Their heads were held high among the green shoots in the field of new wheat. I hesitated as each foot disappeared, sinking into the vertical sea. Charlie followed not far behind me.

I've always felt squeamish walking in tall grass. It is partly the feel of the rough strands brushing against me. But it is also the idea of stepping into the unknown, not being able to see through the grass to what lies ahead, or what might be crawling on the ground just waiting for me to step on it. I stood still and looked at the flowers surrounding me. Each was an individual now, no longer lost in a distant sea of red. The frail petals moved in the wind like silk fabric. I leaned on Charlie's shoulder so James could take a picture, and smiled a lover's smile. It would be the kind of picture you see in travel catalogues – a happy couple laughing in a field of poppies.

Annie was the hike leader for the walk in the steep-sided Gorge du Gardon. James had to shop and prepare our picnic, which he would bring along later. Through the grassy field we followed tracks made and made again by a farmer's tractor. Soon a chalky unpaved road of crushed limestone continued in the brush of the moors of the Garrigue, our hiking place this day. Annie reached for a branch and plucked several narrow pointed leaves, crushing them between her fingers. We did the same and released the familiar scent of thyme. "Rosemary grows wild here also," she said.

Tall shrubs crowded the narrowing road, reaching just above eye level and obstructing any views. When we began to follow a rocky trail downhill I could catch only occasional glimpses of the canyon walls. Annie and I walked side by side.

"So, how does a French gal like you have a name like Annie Wilkins?" I asked her. She had been born in Provence, she told me, and met her husband, an American, at college in Paris. They married and lived in California for five years and when they divorced she started working in Europe as a guide. I asked her why she kept his American name. She shrugged and said, "I like it. I think of it as a symbol of freedom."

She asked about my life, my marriage. I practiced again condensing into a few sentences the story of an eighteen-year marriage, the golden child, a family business, his mid-life crisis and the eager secretary, their out of wedlock child, our divorce and the eventual forgiveness and friendship.

I was walking in front of Annie, looking at my feet as I picked my way down the rocky trail. Annie was quiet, and I thought perhaps I had told her too much. In the years that had passed I was beginning to realize the story made people sad, which was not my intention. It was only a part of my history, a piece like a rough stone in a rushing river, the sharpness being worn away in the water's constant passage downstream.

"Did your husband ever remarry?" I asked.

"Oh yes, a Swiss woman."

I couldn't tell if that was good or bad.

"They have a daughter. Actually, I have remained good friends with him. It's funny, I feel almost like an Aunt to their daughter. She and I would write letters to each other, but his wife got a little jealous, I think. He asked me to stop writing the letters."

Now I felt sad. I wanted to comfort her somehow, this lovely, carefree, vagabond tour guide with a tiny hole in her heart. I liked Annie. We were becoming friends, but I did not feel brave enough to ask her about James.

We had been heading downhill for some time and when I looked up I saw the limestone cliffs of the gorge tumbling down to a ribbon of green, the Gard River. When water is anything other than blue it seems exotic to me.

The sun was high in the sky and it was hot on our shoulders. We followed a path along the cliff and partway down it. I imagined jumping from the rocks, swooping in an elegant swan dive into the river below.

Next we came upon a huge opening in the hillside, the entrance to a cave. Annie said an old hermit had lived there for many years. The walls of the cave curved away from the opening into complete darkness. I fumbled in my pack for matches. They didn't provide much light and burned down to my fingers before I could take more than a few steps. I felt like Becky in *Tom Sawyer*, inching my way along the cool walls of the cave. I stared into the blackness hoping my eyes would adjust, but I could see nothing. If only I'd packed a flashlight, I thought. I wanted to explore this silent cave, the ultimate unknown. Instead I turned and walked back to the bright opening and the safety of company.

I looked down at the river from that hillside and was overwhelmed by its beauty. It curved gently, flat water moving silently below me. Further along the river narrowed and the water tumbled playfully over small rocks in white and turquoise ripples. I felt the wave of this moment and something moved and shifted inside me. It is a feeling of awe and gratitude I've had only when confronted with nature at its most perfect and serene. For me, it is grace.

While the others scrambled down the trail and headed for the shade of the picnic spot, I turned to head on downstream and came to the remains of a small stone house beside the river. Inside I took off my clothes. I had the urge to jump naked into the river nearby, to be baptized in some primitive way, letting the green water slide across my skin. It seemed the only way to make it mine forever.

Fortunately, better judgment overcame my nature girl recklessness and I pulled out my bathing suit and put it on. I sat on the hot rocks with my toes in the water for some time. The willowy shrubs and rocks hid me. When I stood up I could see the others further upstream, gathering for lunch. I pointed my hands over my head and dived, a safe and shallow entry.

"Never, never had nature seemed
to me so touching and so full of feeling."

-Vincent van Gogh

The water was warm and clear and clean, and I swam with long strokes to the other side, crawling onto the beach like a giant lizard. I walked along the bank and waved to the other hikers. I swam slowly back across the river and dressed in the little stone house. This was my own little paradise now. Like the hermit, I could have stayed there forever.

I walked back along the trail thinking only of the river. When I reached our group they were looking at me and laughing. "Look behind you," they said. I turned and saw twenty or thirty elderly hikers just emerging from the trail, following as if I were the Piped Piper. I wondered when they had joined me, quiet elder-shadows.

The newcomers sat down only a few feet from our picnic without the slightest concern that they might be intruding. They pulled out their sandwiches and small containers of food and began eating. Annie spoke to them rapidly in French. They were retired postal workers on a walking holiday, she told us.

The picnic James had prepared was in shambles by now, almost completely devoured before my rejoining the group. The remains were spread across a beautiful red patterned tablecloth. James had artistically arranged his gourmet creations on this background, I could see, but now it appeared as if many small children had randomly smeared his paints with their fingers.

"There's some of that cheese left," Charlie said.

"What about that bread?" Peg asked. "That bread was so good."

"Did you see me swimming?" I asked James, hoping he felt as I did about the river.

"You missed my picnic." He sounded disappointed and annoyed, as if I were his mother and had arrived late to a soccer game. He held knives and large spoons in one hand and began wrapping them in a plain dish-towel. It was too late for me to say, "I'm sorry." For me each day had been a new discovery, but for Annie and James this day, like all previous days, had been planned with care.

We bade farewell to the postal workers, after giving them our remaining salads and cheese, and followed the path along the river downstream. Long terraces of flat rocks layered one on top of the other, jutting into the green water. We hopped across them. Occasionally the group passed a few sunbathers, materialized seemingly out of nowhere. The men joked that they were hoping to see some lovely topless French girls. On the far bank two men stretched across towels, while a third emerged from the water, naked.

When the soft river-edge brush plunged across the rocks to block our way, we were forced into the woods. There the trail was dark green and lush, a welcome relief from the now white-hot heat on the rocks. At last we came to a large clearing with some welcome civilization – a snack bar. We stopped for drinks, Orangina and Coke Light, before continuing down the beach to the canoe and kayak rental shack.

Green canoes stacked one on top of the other in perfect balance. Strewn across the pebble beach near the water's edge was an array of yellow kayaks, the molded plastic types sturdy and easy for beginners to paddle. Each held a small seat and place for your feet, and not much else. It was more like a raft than a boat.

At the rental shack a sandy-haired Frenchman appeared and asked us to try on life preservers. I leaned on the counter for a moment, looking up at the mounds of life jackets hanging across the back wall. When I looked back I saw the Frenchman's eyes. They were pale, a Paul Newman blue, and I had to struggle to look away. His English was laced with such a strong French accent he sounded almost like a cartoon character, PePe LePue or Inspector Clouseau. He handed me an orange life jacket.

"Ah, zees one is for you, just zee right size," he said as he gazed at my chest. We walked down to the beach where James was pulling the kayaks into the water. The Frenchman was openly flirting with me, teasing as he handed me an oar and then pulled it away. I wagged my finger at him as if admonishing a naughty boy and he playfully moved his hand back and forth as if he were slapping my face. Lost in the moment I giggled like a school girl.

"What are you two laughing about?" James looked up from the boats.

"Oh, he's just honing his skills, getting ready for all the American girls that will be here this summer," I answered.

"What?" James snorted, "American girls are easy."

I was stung by his comment. Is that what he really thought – shallow, twittering American girls, suckers for anyone with a foreign accent? He had said it with such authority. How many willing American girls had it taken before he determined we were all "easy"? I remembered my college roommate spending an evening enthralled by her conversation with a Greek exchange-student. After he left, she told me, "That's what I want, a man with an accent."

Maybe she was right. Maybe that's what we all wanted, a little escargot and champagne, a change of pace from a cheeseburger, some shrimp on the barbie and a Foster's beer. I looked at James, but he was busy preparing the boats, dragging the kayaks down to the water. I'd get him back later.

Charlie had asked me at breakfast to share a canoe, but now I wanted to try the kayaks.

"That's okay," Charlie said. "You go with James. I'm going in the canoe."

"No, no, I'm going to take this single one," James replied. "Why don't you and Big John go together?" he said to me. His job now was to navigate us safely down the river.

Early on, James had been the one to give the two Johns the nicknames Big John and Little John. With his gray beard Big John reminded me of Kenny Rogers. I'd seen him from the start as a strong outdoorsman, someone who took fitness seriously. His wife Sue decided to skip the kayaking and ride back to the hotel in the van. As we paddled away from the beach Big John told me he was a member of a rowing team that competed across the United States. I thanked him for letting me share the kayak with him.

"Well, you look pretty well muscled. You should do okay," he said. "Bring the paddle down straight, don't twist it like that. Now pull hard to the left."

As we approached some small rapids he shouted, "Assume ramming speed!" We hit a wave and water poured over the front of the small boat, drenching me. At least it's warm, I thought. I had to concentrate on matching Big John's strokes or risk continuous instruction. Actually, the rapids were a welcome relief. I could sit back for a few seconds and feel the water splash over my legs.

Earlier when swimming in the river I had made the first move, diving in, reaching out, trying to become part of it. Now it was the river's turn. The water came over the bow, playing with me, teasing me, leaving me wet and exhilarated. The yellow kayak bobbed through the waves, like a stick floating down a stream. After each rapid the river widened and the water slowed, becoming flat and calm as if no rapids existed upstream. We pulled alongside James and Big John began splashing water in his direction.

"Water fight!" yelled John. The men scooped the water with their hands, trying furiously to splash each other until, at last, James asked if he'd like to try the single kayak. Big John traded places with James and we watched as he plowed through the water, disappearing around the bend.

"Ah, at last I have you alone," James said, just before Charlie and the other John, Little John, paddled alongside us in their canoe. We drifted side by side. The green water pulled us gently now. There were more bathers along the banks. Small children waded in the shallow spots near shore. I looked up and saw again the magnificent Pont du Gard. We were heading right for it.

"Aqueduct ahead!" James said.

"Oh, are we going under it?" I said.

"Yes, we pull in on the beach on the other side."

"Oh no, you mean it's over?"

Like the roller coaster ride that ends just as you are beginning to enjoy the dips and turns, it was the end of my ride on the tumbling green Gard River.

We arrived back at the Castillon resembling survivors from an accident at sea. My khaki shorts were still soaking wet and I left droplets of water on the carpet in the hallway. I navigated the spiral stairway to the bedroom suite. On a hook behind the bathroom door I found a plush white terry cloth robe. I stripped out of my wet clothes, wrapped the robe around me and collapsed on the bed.

I almost didn't hear the soft knock on the door below. Tightening the belt of the robe, I wound my way down the stairs and opened the door. James, wearing an identical robe, held out two bottles of beer. I took one beer and we went out onto the rooftop terrace. Its single step and red tiles had been baking in the sun. They were warm under our bare feet and we sat side by side on the step. The short stucco walls surrounded us, so from the floor we could just see the edges of the roofs and the blue sky.

"I brought us a little snack left over from the picnic." James opened a small container filled with green olives, swimming in thick olive oil. "I made this from ingredients I picked on the trail today."

I envisioned him dancing in the woods like Pan, the impish Greek god, happily gathering olives from the trees.

"You picked these? I am truly impressed."

"No, not the olives, of course, the herbs in the marinade – the rosemary, the thyme."

"Oh." I said. "Well it's still very impressive." It was bad enough I had missed most of his picnic. "You really worked hard on that picnic, didn't you?"

"Yes, but the worst part was getting everything down to the river."

"Was it heavy?" I asked.

"Yes, it was heavy," he said, mocking me, "all the knives and the wine and the bread board." He raised his eyebrows, "and the whole fucking thing."

Now I pictured him staggering down the rocky trail with an overstuffed backpack, cursing under his breath.

"Well, here's to the river." I said, holding up my beer in its glistening emerald bottle. It was cold and I drank half of it in one gulp. I nibbled the olives and told him how delicious they were. We moved to lie back on the warm tiles, sipping the cold beer, staring at the sky. A perfect moment.

"Let's go upstairs," James said, after a time.

The bedroom loft had been baking in the hot sun all day and the paneled walls gave off the sweet smell of kiln-dried wood. I lay with my head on James's shoulder. The sun had burned his cheeks. His robe was loose and I ran my fingers down his bare chest. His skin was smooth, like a polished stone from the river. "You're like some rare animal found only in Australia," I said playfully, "like a wallaby or a platypus."

He lay on his back with his eyes closed. I could still feel the motion of the river. It was the same feeling I had after spending the day swimming in the waves of the Atlantic Ocean. I was still sliding through the water, but now I was sharing it with James. We stayed in the loft until the sun began to go down. Quiet, peaceful – sharing the time between day and evening.

"Come on," he said as he climbed off the bed. "I want to take a bubble bath with you." He turned on the water in the large tub. He sounded as if he were at the amusement park and did not want to miss any of the rides.

We had known each other for five days, and while I did not think much about it then, I wonder if James realized we had only three days left.

Again, we were already late for dinner when he left my room. I looked in the mirror at my disheveled hair, flying away from my face like Medusa's snakes. I picked up my hairbrush, wondering how to tame snakes in three minutes. The natural waves in my brown hair had been released in this climate. The ends turned up in happy curls, as if to say, "keep that blow-drier away from us."

I ran my fingers through my hair and looked again at my reflection. I liked it. It looked fine, better than fine. I looked wild and free. I threw on silky black pants and a bright blue shirt and tied it at the waist. Carefully I wound myself down the corkscrew stairs and marched across the garden to the lounge.

James looked cool in a starched blue shirt, sipping drinks with the rest of our group. He was a good actor and I doubted if anyone knew what was going on behind the scenes. When I made my entrance I said, "I don't know about you, but this has been one of the top ten days of my life."

Charlie raised his glass as if toasting me, "And it's not over yet."

I drifted through dinner; the wine, the beautiful food, delicately prepared. The group was tired after our physically demanding day and so after our meal, in the darkness of the garden, we disbursed, heading for our rooms. I heard James's voice behind me as I walked toward my door. "I have some work to take care of, but then I'll come on up. I want to see you in some sexy lingerie."

Throughout the trip James had made repeated reference to

the "Lou girl." Whenever we passed near a train station or large highway, he looked for billboards featuring a shapely blonde dressed in lacy Lou lingerie. I remember he liked her best in baby blue.

Now what do I do, I thought as I closed the door. I hadn't packed any sexy lingerie. I had not expected or even hoped for any romance on this trip to France, packing my suitcase with only hiking in mind. My supply of "Jockeys for Her" was not the kind of sexy I thought James was hoping for.

Impulsively I pulled off my thin black pants and removed my panties, tucking them behind a pillow on the sofa. Perhaps no underwear at all was even sexier than lacy Lou lingerie. I thought better of going braless. I had to admit I couldn't carry that off. Before I had a chance to change my mind I heard a knock on the door. James was still dressed in the shirt and pants he'd worn to dinner.

Outside on the terrace we leaned against the wall. The tiles were still warm beneath our feet. The sky was velvet black and the stars little white pinpricks. As we kissed there in the dark his hands ran down my back. They moved as if he were a blind man defining the contours of a statue. He spoke softly, as he kissed my neck, "It feels almost as though you have nothing on underneath." It sounded more like a question than a statement.

"I don't," I whispered.

James took my hand and led me through the French door. As we climbed the stairs to the loft he told me, "You know, Annie was teasing me after dinner. She said 'what were you two doing up there all afternoon . . . one of the ten best days of her life?'"

I laughed, going along with his self-compliment. How could he know it was more than just an afternoon of passion? For me it had been one of those rare days, filled to overflowing with red poppies and warm rivers, dark caves and piercing sunlight, solitude and peace, exertion and exhilaration. And in the darkness there was the uncomplicated comfort found only in the arms of a stranger. No history, no hopes or worries about the future, just a moment of softness, of tenderness before oblivion. Sometime in the night I sent James away, back to his room. The day was over.

By morning a dome of pale gray clouds encased the hilltop of Castillon du Gard. The buds of the flowers in the garden stayed tightly closed, as if they had pulled themselves under their green covers, unwilling to greet the day. The pool that had glistened in the sun now appeared dull. The day before it had been so iridescent it almost seemed to levitate. Now it just lay still on the stone. The magical, crumbling wall with its stairway to nowhere looked like just another ruin.

"Up to now the loneliness has not worried me much because I have found the brighter sun and its effect on nature so absorbing."

-Vincent van Gogh

There was no time to linger after breakfast. I packed and left my room without taking even one last look. The van was full and they were waiting for me, full of anticipation for the day.

We were heading south to Saint Rémy, where Van Gogh had spent a year of his life in an insane asylum. Annie always made sure we drove on country roads, avoiding any glaring evidence of the twentieth century, but as we entered a roundabout I saw massive piles of dirt and jutting cement rails. This, however, was not the remains of another Roman catapult. It was the unfinished construction of a new high speed TGV rail line. For the first time in five days, we were in a traffic jam.

It was market day in Saint Rémy. The streets were lined with colorful tables filled with all manner of products Provençal. James led us to the food stalls and stopped in front of the fishmongers. He began speaking rapidly in French, pointing to what looked like a pile of old rocks covered with dark seaweed. "Ah, *oui*," James said, as the monger picked up one of the crustaceans. He took a knife and cut through the hard shell revealing a gooey orange center. He then cut into the flesh and offered it to James on the end of his knife. After he ate it, James turned to me and said, "Do you want to try some?"

"Where is it from?" I asked, stalling for time.

"The sea," he said, as if he were talking to a child. "We're right near the Mediterranean."

I wanted to appear daring to him, willing to try anything, but this oozing orange slime, raw, not even sitting on ice in the warm marketplace, was more than I could ever imagine eating. Snails? Sure. Brains? Maybe. Even the gently named calf fries (testicles!) I tasted once in Oklahoma. At least they were cooked. But, orange slime from the sea?

If I'd had time to think about it I never would have done it, but James was smiling, waiting. He was the chef. If he thought it was okay, maybe this would be another intimate moment only we would share. No one else in our group wanted to sample this delicacy.

"Mmm, okay," I said, and let the stuff slide into my mouth. The taste was shocking and hideous, like black mud from the bottom of the salty sea. I swallowed it as if it were wretched medicine, just to get rid of it. At the same instant I remembered my sister's tales of swimming in the Mediterranean as a teenager, as she watched unmentionable filth float by. I tried to smile, but it must have looked like a grimace. "Very interesting, but a little metallic," I said, as if I were a food critic. As James rounded the corner, I whispered to Charlie, "I think I've just contracted hepatitis."

For the rest of the morning we jostled among the crowds of locals and tourists. Saint Rémy's market day overtook the entire center of town and beyond. Every inch of sidewalk was crammed with people, tables overflowing with dried lavender bouquets and *herbs de Provence* in large burlap sacks. Older women with baskets held close to their sides pushed past us in search of their next purchase. James gave us general directions and then announced he was off to check us in to our new hotel. At least I wouldn't have to taste any more disgusting food.

Open-air markets are the only kind of shopping I really like. I wandered on my own buying rough-hewn bars of lavender soap and yards of brightly colored fabric with typical Provençal designs. I squeezed past a table overflowing with pale, purple-striped cloves of garlic, stopping to watch the butcher carving a huge carcass of ham. French women leaned over to inspect loaves of fresh baked bread while their miniature dogs peeked out of their handbags. I found the green market and bought a packet of small black seeds. I hoped I could grow the dwarf basil plants James used to decorate his picnics.

I followed the curved streets away from the teaming market and sought refuge in an elegant shop selling home decorations. In my broken French I managed to converse with the owner as I looked for something special to take home. I chose a sachet made from an antique pillowcase filled with fragrant lavender. Embroidered on the thin white linen were the first three letters of the alphabet, A, B, C.

When I was a little girl, about five years old, my mother

made sachets filled with dried lavender we picked together. She showed me how to pinch my fingers around the long stem and pull the purple florets off in one motion. We collected them in a pillowcase. Smells can stir powerful memories. Releasing the scent from lavender crushed between my fingers always leads me back to a summer day and a perennial garden in full bloom.

As the woman in the store was writing my receipt, I saw a small candle in a glass, sitting on a table near the cash register. It had the scent of orange blossoms. I handed it to her. "*Et ça aussi, s'il vous plait.*" She smiled, as if she knew I was imagining candlelight on white pillows in the dark.

I asked her where to have lunch and she told me to go to the café with a green awning. I was content to be alone enjoying my salad with warm goat cheese on slices of toasted baguette. Harried waiters squeezed between the small tables, delivering grilled cheese "*Croc Monsieurs*" and glasses of Cinzano or small cups of espresso. And in my daydream I was living in Saint Rémy.

After my lunch I wandered away from the crowding tourists, down quiet streets. In a square two men sat on the rim of a small, dry fountain, smoking cigarettes. The men were smiling, engrossed in their conversation, and I watched them as if watching a movie.

The fountain was made of simple stone shapes, assembled

like building blocks. There was nothing special about it, no monument to a war hero or Greek goddess, and without water it was little more than a park bench. I was about to move on when I noticed the letters written carefully on the pale stone beyond the men's heads. It was the one piece of graffiti on the fountain and it spelled out my name in black charcoal letters, JENNIFER.

If there had been other words I might not have noticed. My name is a common one now, but when I was a child, the only other person I knew with the name Jennifer was my mother. I was named for her. Oh, there was the movie actress Jennifer Jones and, since my last name was Smith, people, would say, "Oh, Jennifer Smith, like Jennifer Jones? Smith, Jones, same difference." My friends were all named Cathy and Sarah and Bonnie. My name was unusual then, one more thing that made me feel different, along with my brown and white striped horn-rimmed glasses. People have tried to give me nicknames. My siblings still use the diminutive, almost masculine Jen, but I never adopted any of the non-Jennifer names. And now James called me Jenny, a new name with its own sweet innocence and daring.

When my marriage ended, my given name became an important symbol to me. Not my father's name, or my husband's, just Jennifer. With my new freedom I have chosen to

"There is a sun, a light that for want of a better word I can only call yellow, pale sulphur yellow, pale golden citron. How lovely yellow is!"

-Vincent van Gogh

travel, not to escape but as a way to find pieces of myself I had lost along the way. On that small fountain in Saint Rémy de Provence, written in charcoal, was a simple indication I was in the right place. I did not know how it got there, I wasn't even curious. The anonymous writer would never know what his black scribbling meant to a stranger named Jennifer.

At two o'clock we met on the steps of Eglise St. Martin to begin our walk to St.-Paul-de-Mausole, the asylum where Van Gogh came to recover after cutting off a piece of his ear.

We walked in silence along the road to the outskirts of town. It was a warm afternoon in May, the same month Van Gogh had arrived here, making the same trip down the long driveway. On one side of the drive, against the backdrop of the blue Alpilles Mountains, stood a grove of olive trees. The dry grass between the trunks had not been mowed and the trees looked as if they had been there a long time. I realized with a shock of recognition. Olive trees. These were the same olive trees Van Gogh painted while living at the asylum.

On either side of the entrance two fat cypress trees stood guard. Originally a monastery, the place was still quiet and peaceful, no hint of frightening institution. Inside the cloister a courtyard garden had been carefully planted with pansies framed in geometric patterns by diminutive boxwood. Baskets of red and purple bleeding hearts and trailing vinca hung in the corners. I could see why Van Gogh did not want to leave. He had been comforted by understanding nuns and had created more than one hundred fifty paintings during the single year he spent here.

We saw his room on the second floor and I looked through the small window at his view. It was from this window that he had painted one of his visions of a starry night. His presence must linger here, I thought, an inspiration for today's patients. The place is still an asylum, but now there is an art therapy center – perhaps a reflection of the solace he found at St.-Paul-de-Mausole.

As we walked back down the driveway, I looked again at the olive grove. Had Van Gogh walked through this field and stood in the tall grass while he painted the twisted trees? Or had he looked out his window and tried to capture the scene? He painted and drew them so many times. Was it the rhythmic shapes of the gnarled branches that intrigued him? Or did he just want a picture so he could remember this peaceful place?

I was staring at the trees when Charlie walked up behind me. "We are so accustomed to recognizing places from photographs," I said. "It's amazing to recognize a place from a painting."

James led us across the road to Les Antiques, two impressive monuments erected eons ago by the Romans. The

"I absolutely want to paint a starry sky.
It often seems to me that night is still more richly
coloured than the day."

-Vincent van Gogh

Triumphal Arch and the Mausoleum were over two thousand years old and had somehow withstood the mistral and other Provençal winds, and other tests of time and weather. The Mausoleum is actually a memorial to Caesar and the structures had decorated the end of the Roman road from Arles to Glanum. After the serenity of the olive grove these grand "landmarks" looked strangely out of place. I could see locals referring to them when giving directions. "Turn right five hundred feet past Les Antiques."

James waved and smiled as a neatly dressed woman approached us. This was Hélène, our local guide for the ruins of Glanum. She was very pretty and wore a gray suit with a short skirt and a tight blouse. Her jewelry was big, a gold necklace and bright earrings. Dressed in her high heels she looked more like one of the ladies who lunch than a guide to an archeological site. Her brown hair was smooth against her head, tied with a patterned silk scarf. Standing on the grass, surrounded by our group of Americans in shorts and sneakers, it was she who looked strangely out of place. I saw James elbow Charlie and give him a "boys will be boys" look.

Hélène led us through the small museum and down a sandy path to the remains of the town. Low walls about a foot high constituted the remains – mere outlines of buildings – and with enough imagination, we were told, we could picture a thriving civilization there. The town had been built by the Greeks as a miniature Pompeii, but in the hot sun I felt I was seeing one Roman ruin too many. I looked around desperately for shade. We followed Hélène, politely, through the baths, the toilets, the brothel. When she asked, "Does anyone have a question?" no one said a word. And I was grateful.

Early on, James came and stood close to me the way he had at the Palais des Papes in Avignon. I waited to feel something and then turned to him and smiled. Nice try, I thought, but it's not the same.

We left Hélène in the hot sun and followed the road leading to our next hotel. Charlie walked next to James and I heard him say, "Have you had her as a guide before, James?" Charlie chuckled, "maybe she's free tonight. She's certainly a very attractive woman."

"Yeah, but Charlie, I always try to stay clear of the warning lights."

It took me a minute to figure out he meant her jewelry.

L'Hôtel Les Antiques sat like a withering mushroom behind a high stone wall, sheltered from the traffic on the main road entering Saint Rémy. A tall wooden-planked door slid on wheels across the tiny beige pebbles at the driveway entrance. At night the door would be pulled shut, sequestering the guests. This was another faded manor house which, for whatever sad reasons, had been haphazardly converted to a hotel. I remember only pieces of my first impression – the crunch of loose stones as we filed to front steps, cool, dark marble floors and a marble counter, the clunky wooden key ring and climbing the wide crescent stairway. My room was in *chambre quatre*, room number four, left at the end of a short hallway.

The room was blue, baby blue. The faded lacy wallpaper looked like fabric from a Victorian wedding dress, a gown hanging in the back of an attic closet, abandoned but not forgotten by its once young owner. The room was small, and closing the door I faced two large windows with plain organdy curtains through which I could see a high wall protecting the garden from the main road. There was one bed, a small double. I sat down and lay back on crisp white pillows.

It was then that I saw it for the first time. Centered above the bed on the ceiling was an old painted fresco. It was oval, a blue sky with puffy clouds. Two pink cherubs floated above me. They were relief sculptures, emerging in half-life from the sky, their plump hands reaching playfully for each other. This would have been a handmaiden's room when Marie Antoinette lived in the Palace of Versailles.

The phone rang, interrupting my daydream.

"Ah, *Bonjour, Madame*. Eeez everything all right with your

room?" I laughed at James mimicking a French accent.

"Yes, it's great."

"I wasn't sure which room to give you. I kept switching the bags back and forth. The one at the other end of the hall is bigger, but it's brown and I didn't think you'd like that."

"But this one has the cherubs on the ceiling." I was sure I was the only one with that little glimpse into heaven.

"Is it okay if I come down?"

"Of course. I was just resting."

"I'll see you in a few minutes." He paused, like an actor getting into character, and purred, "*A bientôt*," a promise that flowed through the phone like thick, sweet syrup. See you soon.

"Are you sure you like it? It's certainly not as nice as Le Vieux Castillon." James seemed embarrassed about the shabbiness of the hotel.

"No, but it's different. Maybe it has some mysterious history. And I have never slept underneath cavorting cherubs before," I said.

"Well, you can add that to your list, eh?"

We spent the rest of that lazy afternoon under the cherubs. As the fading sun streamed through the windows James knelt above me and said, "My God, look at you. If you look like this now, what must you have been like at twenty-five?"

I did not take his remark as an insult, but as an invitation to act as if I were twenty-five, to pretend in this dreamlike place that I was that young woman I abandoned long ago. Pushing him back on the pillows I whispered, "Now you can look at the cherubs." My hands on his chest were all that grounded me as I floated off into the fresco sky. My eyes were closed and he must have known I was far away.

"Look at me," he said as he reached up and put his fingers in my mouth. I closed my eyes again only when I bit down slightly to stifle a cry.

Afterwards, when he drifted into sleep, I looked at my hand on the white sheet. Twenty-five. Almost half a lifetime ago. At twenty-five my mother was dying of cancer and I was planning my wedding. After our years of fighting it was the least I could do. I didn't think a mother's life should end without seeing at least one of her daughters get married.

In the last six months of her life I became the good dutiful daughter. My mother chose a traditional wedding gown for me and I walked down the aisle thinking I was doing the right thing.

Being married would solve all my problems, be my ticket out of aimless confusion. I would put the wild child in me to bed without supper and would gain a proper identity and direction. I would be a wife and then a mother.

Now, on my own all these years later, making love with an Australian somewhere in France, I remembered the words from *My Back Pages*, a song from my bygone hippie days. "I was so much older then, I'm younger than that now." We'd made fun of The Byrds when we'd heard those lyrics on the radio, dressed in our bell-bottoms and peace beads. "Wow, that's really deep," we'd mocked. But that was before I was an old woman at twenty-five and a younger one at forty-eight.

James stirred. "What time is it?" he asked.

"It's about quarter to five," I said.

"Oh, shit. I've got to go buy the stuff for tomorrow's picnic." He was already up and getting dressed. He looked at me over his shoulder. "Do you want to come?"

It was the first time he'd asked me to go somewhere that was not part of the itinerary. As I crossed the floor, heading for the bathroom, he grabbed me and spun me to face him. His brown eyes had softened to the color of good Scotch, and he looked at me, vaguely surprised. "I've never met anyone quite like you before," he said.

"Ah, but you see, my dear James," I laughed. "That is because you have come across a Woman of Substance."

He cocked his head, smiling and not understanding.

I wished I hadn't said it. It made me sound like an aging

matron, making a desperate ploy to stand out amongst the others in his memory. "Oh, it's just something I do every summer," I said, trying to recover. "A group of my women friends get together every year for what I call the Annual Women of Substance Dinner. The first year we had so many bottles of champagne we thought we should rename it the women of substance abuse dinner."

He laughed, "I'd like to be a fly on the wall at one of those."

"Maybe not," I said, closing the door behind me.

James was waiting for me in the van. I ran across the fine stones of the driveway and hopped in the front seat. As we turned onto the main road I looked back over my shoulder at the empty seats. Riding alone in the van with James felt wonderfully illicit.

"Do you have a coin, a franc? We're going to need it for the trolley," James said.

"Aren't we driving to the market?" I asked.

"Yes, but we need the trolley when we get there."

"We need a trolley when we get there?" I couldn't imagine what he was talking about. We were just going to buy groceries. "Why do we need a trolley?"

"You know, to put the food in as we go around the store."

"Oh, you mean the cart."

"My God," he said as he turned the corner. "It's like speaking a whole other language."

Except for the Peugeots and the tiny Citroëns the supermarket parking lot looked like any in America. As we wheeled the shopping cart, the trolley, through the produce section, James became the chef, carefully examining each head of lettuce, squeezing melons. I was surprised to see the miniature basil plants lined up like Christmas poinsettias. "Is this where you get them?" I asked, but he had moved on, busy now caressing and selecting the perfect tomato.

We passed the French version of the deli counter, but there was no bologna or creamy white potato salad. Instead twenty different types of paté sat lined up in white ceramic tureens. James asked the young girl for a slice from a large wheel of Roquefort cheese. It was clear his sampling was going to take awhile.

"Can you go find a small jar of cornichons?" he asked me, at the same time pointing to another hunk of cheese. "What?" The confused look on my face gave me away.

"Little pickles," he explained.

I passed a refrigerated case filled with vacuum-sealed packages of mussels and tongue and rabbit and oysters. With the jar of little pickles in hand, I found James gathering several bottles of wine. "Here," he said, pushing the loaded cart toward me,

"Can you take this to the checkout while I run and get some sweets?"

I had placed the last jar of Dijon mustard in front of the cashier when he appeared behind me. "Look at this pile of food," I said. "Do you really think we'll eat all this in one picnic?"

"This is how much you guys have been eating every day."

Back at the hotel, James divided the bags and asked if I would keep the smelly packages of cheese in my mini bar refrigerator. We had reached a new level of intimacy. I said yes. There was no time to discuss it. We were due at dinner in fifteen minutes.

When I rushed across the street to our restaurant I found James sitting casually between Annie and Peg at the long table. Annie always managed to look lovely at these dinners, just the right mixture of femininity and rough-and-ready adventurer. Tonight she wore her long brown hair down so that it fell below her shoulders, meeting the folds of a red cotton scarf. She had what seemed genetic in French women: style, cachet, they called it *prêt à porter*, ready for anything. Peg and Sue wore their never-need-ironing knits designed for the American traveler.

In the fading light we were the only diners out on the restaurant terrace. I felt it was my job to provide the entertainment. "Well, I had an exciting afternoon," I announced as I sat down. I saw James inhale slowly and hold his breath.

"What did you do?" asked Charlie, acting the perfect foil.

"I got to watch the master at work," I said.

Annie stared at me. From across the table I saw James smile, accepting the compliment, but he also gave me a look of caution. Earlier he had confided it was against company policy for guides to fraternize with clients. "You are the exception," he had told me.

"I went to the supermarket with James," I confessed, watching James laugh, relieved.

Maybe our group was tired as the trip neared its final days, or maybe we had learned as much as we wanted about each other. But the conversation over dinner was forced, degenerating into a discussion of the derivation and choices of children's names. I was impatient, not just because I wanted to be with James, but to see what would happen next.

I felt myself shedding hardened layers of protection. Romance did that. But there was more. This stronger sun softened me. I felt the colors of flowers, emotions stirred by their very existence. Maybe this was the French *joie de vivre*. These forced dinner conversations intruded upon my private experience of Provence.

As it grew dark outside at last, the spring air chilled and we took turns running back to the hotel for sweaters. Inside, the restaurant glowed with warm yellow light and the muted voices of sophisticated diners just arriving. On the terrace we were the ugly Americans. For the French, the evening was young. The waiter brought the check, practically shooing us away. Hurry along now, children, he might have said, this is the grown-ups' party.

In our hotel's small lobby I approached the marble counter to retrieve my room key. The others had wandered into the sunroom overlooking the garden. I was wondering how I would spend the rest of the night when I felt James next to me. Quietly he said, "Would you like to walk into town and have an Armagnac at one of the cafés?" I nodded and he added, "I'll meet you in the drive."

I wandered into one of the drawing rooms, with its dark velvet settees and gilt chairs and stared without interest at the paintings. When I was sure no one was looking, I walked through the lobby and down the steps of the hotel.

James was standing next to the opened door of the van. Annie was sitting inside in the dark, bent over her glowing laptop. They were working, their heads together, making plans for the next group they would lead through the hills of Provence. These soon-to-be-known travelers who existed in the future would be here with James and Annie. It was an acrid reminder that I would before long be part of the past.

"Do you know what I hope for, once I allow myself begin to hope? It is that the family will be for you what nature, the lumps of soil, the grass, the yellow wheat, the peasant, are for me, in other words, that you find in your love for people something not only to work for, but to comfort and restore you when you need it."

-Vincent van Gogh

When Annie saw me she said, "You two better get going. I saw John wandering around looking for someone to go for a walk." James quickly turned and gave me his mischievous elf smile and without a word, ran out the driveway. He slowed for a moment to look back at me, holding his head sideways, still smiling, high stepping like a circus clown as he ran on down the street. Annie continued shuffling intently through her papers. I turned and ran down the street after James.

Whatever romantic fantasies I ever had about France, they are embodied in French cafés. Their images so distinctive, to me the cafés themselves were characters from novels. They were the smoky haunts of famous painters and writers. Even the prostitutes were mysterious and appealing in cafés. Along the streets of Paris, every one seemed filled with lovers or with men and women waiting to meet lovers. Whenever I had tried to sit and sip a glass of red wine I had felt awkward, out of place, American.

James stopped running as soon as he reached the place where the street curved, flowing into the town of Saint Rémy. The cafés were quiet. Perhaps it was too early in the evening or just early in the season. We walked together across the street, trying to choose. Blue chairs, green chairs, red chairs. The gray haired proprietor of the red chairs smiled at us, the knowing

French smile, and extended his hand like an opera singer hitting his final note. It was an expression I had seen before, "Ah lovers, yes, we welcome lovers here."

We sat in the back row of tiny tables and James ordered two Armagnacs. The waiter brought small brandy snifters glowing with amber liquid. James made the liquor swirl, like little whirlpools. He took a sip, and as he turned his head I turned mine, an intuitive reflex that lovers share. When our lips touched I felt the Armagnac burn as it flowed from his mouth to mine. "You should always warm the Armagnac before you drink it," he said.

We sat there, looking out, each waiting. James broke our silence. "Annie told me about how your marriage ended." He was trying to sound like a confidant and not a conspirator. I looked down into my lap. "I try not to talk about it anymore," I said.

"Why, because it's so painful?"

"No, that part is over," I lied. "It's just . . ." I remembered the look on Annie's face when I recited the condensed version. Discomfort is what we were taught to call it in child-birthing class. And there had been something else, a cloud of sadness, or was it closer to pity? "It's just that now, I see how others react to it," I said. "It's not a pleasant story."

Seven years earlier the drink had been Scotch, not Armagnac. My husband handed me the glass as I lay on our bed. He came home late from the office, but that had become routine. I was in our son's room reading to him, our bedtime ritual, when Ben came into the room. He had that sad look I had been trying to ignore. I left them alone so he could kiss his son goodnight.

When he slouched into our bedroom he pushed the glass of Scotch into my hand.

"Why are you giving me this?" I'd asked. "It's eleven thirty."

It was the first Friday in March.

"I have something I need to tell you."

Not want to tell you, but need to tell you.

And then a blur and my brain shutting down, hearing only key phrases . . . "three and a half years ago . . . an affair . . ."

My mind provided a silent narration under his confession.

. . . Okay . . . probably some colleague's secretary in New York . . . it's over now, right?

And his voice again pushing through, "There's a child, a daughter."

I remember sitting up in bed, clamping my hands over my ears and saying, "I don't want to hear this."

And then, saving him from having to choose the words, asking, "Who is it? . . . not she, but it, and the flood of numbing reality in his one-word answer, "Patrice."

I had been the one to hire Patrice as a clerk. Ten years ago she came to work in our office, opening mail. Soon she was an executive working with not only my husband, but also my father and mother-in-law in the family business. When our son was born I stayed home, but I would frequently stop in at the office. I remember once seeing a bouquet of roses on Patrice's desk. They were lavender, the most unusual roses I'd ever seen, and I asked if it was her birthday. She said no and then smiled. I remember asking her how her pregnancy was going, and then about the baby. "Do you have a picture?" I once asked. I had been surprised when she said no. And when my husband said that no one knew who the father was, I never pushed. I believed him.

The memory of his midnight confession comes back to me now only in a brief flash. Like the big green barn door I have forgotten to close, it hangs unnoticed until a gust of wind grabs it and throws it open violently against the wall. And then it drifts back, suspended silently until I close it and secure the latch.

I'm not sure how much of the story I told James. I heard his voice asking, "Did they ever get married?"

In one long breath the word "No" flowed out of me. "I asked him once when he realized they were not going to ride off into the sunset together. He told me, 'Pretty much as soon as you and I separated.' But she still works there."

James looked at me surprised, the way others had. She still works there. It is one of the two realities that will not go away.

"I told you about my son," James was now saying, "but I also have a daughter."

It was his turn to confess.

"She is eight years old now."

I thought of Ben and Patrice. "Everyone in the world has a daughter who is eight," I sighed.

He looked at me, but continued his story. For Australians, England can be like a second home, returning to the mother who cast them out. James had made it his second home for a time, or maybe more of a waystation between guiding trips in Europe or Nepal. Now there was a little girl with his pale skin and dark hair who owned a permanent place in his heart. I could hear the mixture of emotions in his voice.

"You should have seen me sitting at my parents' kitchen table crying my eyes out, when I told them," he said.

We sat in silence in the deserted café. "I'm sorry I didn't tell you earlier about my daughter," James said finally.

All I could say was, "Why?"

The Armagnac was strong and I was glad. I don't think my mind was clear enough then to grasp the extraordinary chronological similarity in our separate lives. James and I had sons the same age, and those sons had half sisters the same age. It was like one of those math puzzles on an IQ Test. "If James and Jennifer leave Chicago at the same time, and James is traveling at fifty miles an hour . . . and James has never married and has a son born the same year as Jennifer's son, and Jennifer's husband has a daughter the same age as James's daughter while they were married, what is the relationship between James and Jennifer?" It made my head spin.

I swirled the last of the Armagnac and felt it warm my throat as I finished it. Whatever happened in the past could not smother the glow of romance in Saint Rémy.

We left the café and walked hand in hand on the quiet street. L'Hôtel Les Antiques now appeared a little sad in the hazy blue streetlight. James followed me to my room and did not ask if he could stay. We went to bed as if we had known each other a very long time.

Sometime in the night I awoke feeling sick. I had never really gotten over that first bout of food poisoning. When I realized James was beside me, I tried to move silently from the bed into the bathroom. I did not want him to see me sick.

"Are you all right?" he asked.

"No, I think you better go."

"But I want to take care of you. I can nurse you," he said.

"No, please, let me be alone."

"I'm going to get you some pills from Nepal." He returned with white tablets and a glass of water. "Are you sure you won't let me stay?" he asked.

"No, let me try to get some sleep."

James kissed me on my cheek. I heard him close the door and tiptoe down the hall.

When the alarm rang I felt I'd been asleep for just a few minutes. But morning light was streaming through the lace curtains and it was time for breakfast.

I believe in feeding not only a cold but also a fever – or any ailment, for that matter. I wore sunglasses hoping to cover my bloodshot eyes. I could get away with it since breakfast was served on the outdoor terrace. I continued my pattern of avoiding James in the morning. It felt too intimate and I still imagined our extracurricular activities were unknown to the rest of the group. I sat down next to Charlie and managed to croak "Good morning" to Peg and Tim.

"You don't sound too good," Charlie said.

"I think all the wine is catching up with me." I ordered tea instead of coffee and spread the lavender honey on a plain roll, hoping it would be medicinal as well as magical. But the roll tasted like cotton and too soon it was time to leave.

Our walk this morning would be along the rocky crest of the Chaine des Alpilles. These low mountains were the background for Van Gogh's olive trees, for the fields he painted, for his cypress trees. Les Alpilles were his horizon. It was our turn now to climb above the dark green forests and weave our way through the white spires to the Col de la Vallonge.

The fields at the trailhead were wild-rough tufts of overgrown brown weeds and grass. The ever-present poppies were scattered small dots of brilliant red. At the edge of the field, a solid mass of cypress trees appeared almost black in the morning shadows. It was still so dark that at first I did not see him, a single white horse in the shade, looking across the field at me. Alas, there was no sign of Prince Charming. And James had driven off to prepare our picnic.

I was in no condition to hike, but nevertheless methodically put one foot in front of the other on the dirt road. Annie was cheerful until we came to a crossroads. She turned in circles, examining large rocks, trying to remember the way. Finally she called to us, *"Allez, les enfants."*

We continued on and I was grateful the trail was now leading downhill, but after awhile Annie started talking to herself. "Maybe we should have gone left back there," I heard her say. We met other hikers on the trail and she spoke to them in

French, asking directions. When we rounded the curve in the road, we were back where we started.

"Oh, no," I groaned.

"What's wrong with you today?" Charlie asked. From the first day, we had walked the same pace on the trails and enjoyed each other's company. We had become permanent hiking buddies. I couldn't tell him about James, and late nights and Armagnac. Maybe I could blame it on the shellfish I ate in the market.

"How long do you think it takes for hepatitis to incubate?" I asked.

"I don't think you have hepatitis," he chuckled, his tone dismissive, devoid of comfort.

We climbed past the crossroads again and stopped to rest under some pine trees. I immediately lay down on the ground, using my pack as a pillow. The shade felt good and the water helped, but I'd have been happy to stay there for the rest of the afternoon.

When we continued, the trail leveled into a dirt road on flat ground. This was the crest of Les Alpilles, but the waist-high bushes and wind-blown pines extended endlessly on either side of the road so there was no view. I let the group get ahead of me. The sun was hot, but I was happier alone, watching my feet make small dust clouds in the dry dirt.

I walked this way for awhile, almost in a dream. When I looked up, four men on horseback, like a mirage, were riding toward me. In my heat-induced daze I stared at them, thinking how nice it would be to be on horseback myself, just like the time I was ten years old, bareback on a pinto pony, riding along the dirt road called the racetrack at Eaton's ranch in Wyoming.

The men passed alongside of me. Each rider smiled and each said, "*Bonjour.*" Four French cowboys, smiling and saying *Bonjour*. I wanted to freeze the picture in my memory and turned to look at them again. The last rider had his hand on the back of his saddle, his head turned, watching me. I smiled as our eyes met, and he held my gaze, forcing me to turn away first.

I was still smiling when I rounded the bend and saw Peg waiting for me. When I told her about the four horsemen of Provence and the penetrating eyes of the last rider, Peg said, "Oh yes, I read about that in a book. It was called *French or Foe*. There was an entire chapter devoted to it. They called it The Look."

Once again, I was the victim of a cliché.

The chalky peaks of Les Alpilles were beginning to poke through the mounds of vegetation, so that the only colors were shades of green and white. Now the path twisted and turned and the rocks grew into huge castles, piled high, giant building blocks balanced precariously. Tenacious junipers grew in the crags of the porous limestone formations. Whether they are small smooth stones or giant slabs, I always find comfort in the strength and permanence of rocks. They hold the heat of the sun and the secrets of time.

Nestled in this surreal landscape, under the shade of a sparse pine tree, James had laid out his picnic. The packages of food from the shopping cart the day before were arranged carefully on the red patterned tablecloth, like an artist's still life. At one end a ceramic crock held a starburst of baguettes. Round slices of tomatoes were arranged like flowers, a dark center of olive tapenade for their stamen. There were salads and cheeses and patés and chilled bottles of wine. If I had been alone with James, it would have been perfect. Instead of making small talk I could have been lying with my head in his lap, lazy and content, while he fed me delicious mouthfuls of his feast.

After lunch we drove to Les Baux de Provence, the famous citadel carved out of solid rock. From the car-park we followed the signs and other tourists climbing the streets of the village. Inevitably, en route to this and other historic sights we had to pass through the familiar gauntlet of souvenir shops. I picked up a colorful pouch filled with lavender and held it close to my nose, smelling the fragrance, in what had by now become a reflex action. "You can't even move on these streets in the middle of summer," James said. "We're lucky it's May."

At the top of the town stood the entrance to Les Baux itself. Surprisingly, very few people made it this far. The flat summit spread out, and crushed white rocky paths led to the ruins of this *"Ville Morte."* In America we would call it a ghost town.

Settled since the Stone Age, Les Baux was flanked by sheer cliffs on three sides of its barren plateau, making it a place of awe and evil. It had been a medieval stronghold, a seat of influence in the Middle Ages. As we passed the famed giant catapult we heard stories of dissidents being thrown from the highest rocks to their deaths hundreds of feet below.

We climbed stone stairs on the remaining outside wall of the castle and at the very top took in the view from an arched window. The hills below were covered with olive groves laid out in neat rows, a pattern of green and red clay earth divided sporadically by lines of nearly black cypress trees. Row after row, the patchwork dissolved into a blue haze on the horizon. I rested my arms on the edge of the stone blocks and leaned over the edge.

"That would be a nice spot to have a little country home, eh?" said James, "a *maison secondaire*, or would it be a *maison troisième* for you?"

His comment felt like prying, and I didn't answer him. I wasn't sure how much I wanted him to know about how I lived when I wasn't traveling. I had an old house on a hill surrounded by tall pine trees. I cared for it and in good and bad times it was my place of comfort. James and I both knew we led different lives. He said he was known as the man who would never say, "Home, James." Leading people from place to place was his life – the world was his home.

When we returned to the hotel I reread the itinerary. The evening was listed as "free, to maximize your dining opportunities." I'm sure for couples on these trips it's a wonderful idea, but I have yet to master the art of dining alone. I can handle breakfast and lunch, but dinner alone remains a terror worse than rappelling off a mountaintop. No culinary delights could make up for condescending waiters, an empty table and silence.

James knocked on the door. It was our last leisurely afternoon. He liked to tell jokes and we were lying on the bed laughing when he asked, "What do you have to do when you get home?" I was not ready for the intrusion of reality. I could tell him anything, for he was not part of my life as a mother, a friend, a writer. Not yet.

"I'm working on an article about rooftop gardens," I said.

"I've been in some newspaper articles myself," he told me, and with great enthusiasm described biking across northern England, stopping to stay with his friend who worked for the local paper. "He was all worried about his deadline," James said, "But I just wanted to sit around and party."

I could see these two overgrown boys, laughing, drinking in pubs, telling tales.

"I told him about my ride and this little roadside stand I had stopped at to get fish and chips," James continued. "It was so cheap, fish and chips and mushy peas for 99p."

"But how did it taste?" I asked.

"Pretty good, for that price." He didn't say how many beers they drank before his friend decided this would be the perfect story for the local newspaper. The next day they returned to the snack stand and took a photograph of James on his bike. The story and photograph appeared on the front page with the caption, "Chef James says, 'Fish and chips and mushy peas, best bargain in Europe!'"

James held up his hands for emphasis. "Front page. Not bad, eh?"

Often in those last days James looked at me as if he were mulling over some deep question. And then he would smile, amused by his own secret thoughts. Lying on the bed in the late afternoon light he watched me get up and cross the room. "You know, I feel as if you have been out there my whole life and I've just been waiting to meet you."

Even in the midst of romance it sounded like a line from a movie. Tom Hanks must have said it somewhere to Meg Ryan. I did not want to be so cynical, but I'd heard these movie lines before. Perhaps I was instinctively preparing for my safety, my protection from the parting soon to come.

Later as I stood by the window he held me, his arms around my waist and said, "Oh, do you really have to leave the day after tomorrow?"

I sensed this was an oft-repeated question, almost like a Game Show, requiring a correct response. I had heard it before, too, in a different setting. The pony-tailed rock climber in Chile had asked me on our last night, "Can't you stay? We could travel around together." And I was cool then when I told him, "It's better this way, don't you think?"

But sometimes I wondered what adventure I might have passed up. So now I deviated from the safe script and said, "Well, I have a ticket, but maybe it could be changed." I felt something inside James tighten. He pulled up slightly, as if he felt a small stone in his shoe, and then recovering, said softly, "I think it's always best to leave wanting more."

I felt my tongue press against the roof of my mouth, holding back my breath for a moment. I was angry, but not at James. I knew the rules of this game. When would I learn not to leave myself vulnerable? I was like a wolf in battle that lies on her back and bares her throat. I looked away, not wanting him to see the shadow fallen across my eyes. It was a familiar ache, once an unbearable ache I had learned to bear.

"My God, it's five o'clock," he said. "I'm supposed to go with Annie to check out a new restaurant for tomorrow night. Would you like to come?" I forced myself back to the reality of the moment, the respect for the rules.

James picked up the phone and rang Annie's room. I liked the idea of being treated as a friend of theirs. I pictured the three of us laughing together in the van. James looked at me and began to apologize, "I wish I could take you, but Annie says it's meant to be a surprise." I was not their friend. I was a client and Annie knew it. He pulled his shirt over his head. "But do you want to go with me for dinner later? It'll be pretty late, maybe nine o'clock."

I pretended it didn't matter. I had to pack anyway.

After he left, it occurred to me this would be our first dinner alone, our first true date. Well, he was from Australia, the upside down, other half of the world. Maybe they did things differently there.

Waiting. I have always feared that the ability to wait was a discipline, an acquired skill one could learn, if only one set one's mind to it. There had to be a trick to waiting, a way to just slide through it without feeling like jumping out of your skin. It is a secret I have never discovered, whether the wait is only minutes or hours – or the long-term variety, the kind of waiting that floats around for months or years, holding the future hostage.

I remember as a teenager, waiting in front of Bloomingdale's to meet my father. For forty-five endless minutes I stood at one end of the block, while he stood at the other, waiting. Afraid to move, for that would be the exact second he might appear, I suffered every symptom of low-grade panic. When we finally found each other, I felt it was I only who had done something wrong.

After James left the room, I thought about his comment, leaving wanting more. He was already becoming a memory, with a beginning and an end. Tomorrow would be the last full day.

I used the waiting time to deal with the odious task of packing. The dusty pants worn on the trail in Les Alpilles, the blue bathing suit, sweaty tee shirts, all were thrown in the bottom of the suitcase. I covered them with the neatly folded yards of blue and red fabrics I had bought in the market.

I did not want to think about leaving, not because I didn't want to think about going home. I did not want to think about the moment of leaving. Each day had been filled with unpredictability. It had kept me on edge, without time for idle fantasies. Alone with James I had begun to feel as if we were playing scenes from old movies. The words he said sounded vaguely familiar and he acted as if he knew it and made no excuses. It was in the script. I enjoyed my role and would be ready for the ending. I just wished the closing scene could be spontaneous.

As the afternoon light turned to dusk, I lay on the bed and stared at the cherubs on the ceiling, wondering what it would be like to float away as easily as they. The sky darkened and the room took on the cool blue cast of street lamps. I closed my eyes and slept, or maybe I was just waiting.

When James phoned my room I answered with, "Oh, are you back already?" The one trick I have learned is never let them know you've been waiting.

"How did you and Annie like the restaurant?" I asked as we walked down the quiet street in Saint Rémy.

"Oh, it's fantastic. It's quite a ways out in the country. The woman who owns it took quite a fancy to me, I think. She let me come into the kitchen, and," he turned to look at me, "I think she might even prepare *lapin* for us." I thought of my father and how he might react to the idea of eating little bunnies. He refused to eat lamb because he couldn't bear to think of the fuzzy little creatures being slaughtered.

"There's a place down here we could try." James said, turning off the main street.

I was half running to keep up with him. On the narrow sidewalk I was forced to follow behind him. The restaurant was pink and flowery, the kind of place a tour guide might describe as romantic. Outside the front door a large menu listed their delicacies of the evening along with a costly *prix fixe*.

"I don't know." James shrugged his shoulders. "Let's try someplace else."

We were now traveling down the small streets leading away from the charming shops and cafés one reads about in travel guides. We passed a tiny garage with a pile of crumpled Citroëns waiting to be repaired. "The one place I really wanted to take you, well, I think the others are probably there too," James said.

He was walking on the sidewalk and I was now in the street, looking up at him. We stopped in front of a wooden stockade fence, the kind used to control snowdrifts on open fields. Hanging from the fence was a hand-written menu for the evening meal.

"Shall we try this place?" James said.

Inside the fence several small tables were arranged for dining al fresco. A round-faced man appeared in the doorway to the restaurant. His cheeks were pink as if roughened by sandpaper. He looked a bit like the local butcher who had just removed his bloodied apron, exchanging it for a clean white one. He was happy to see us, smiling, pointing to the empty tables.

There were a few voices inside, and through the doorway I could see the dark brown glow of a pub. We sat at a table outside. Along the fence bright-colored lights hung draped like swags of garland. They looked like Christmas lights someone had forgotten to take down. But these were round, the size of golf balls, and their primary colors had an innocence, like a child's yellow dump truck abandoned in the sandbox. On the table a candle flickered in its wine bottle covered with rivulets of wax drippings.

A young girl with long brown hair soon appeared from behind the white apron of the round-faced owner. She shyly placed two menus in front of us and then backed way from the table.

James studied the menu as if reading a textbook. He was not a diner looking for what might satisfy his hunger or taste. He read between the lines, analyzing the ingredients and trying to interpret the intention of the chef. It took him a long time to choose.

The only item on the menu I recognized was *Coquilles St. Jacques*. My mother had a skill for cooking not passed on to me.

She had grown up in Brooklyn, the daughter of a widowed Polish immigrant. When she married my father, she took cooking classes at the Cordon Bleu School in New York. She loved to show off, preparing exotic dishes for guests. *Coquilles St. Jacques* was one of her favorites. I remember her saying the words, the way they rolled off her tongue, as if she were the perfect French linguist. She even bought the large flat scallop shells so her presentation would be authentic. My sisters and I later used the shells as soap dishes.

The girl returned to our table with a bottle of red wine.

"I'll have *Coquilles St. Jacques*," I said, absently.

"And I think I am going to have the tripe," James said, asking several questions about its preparation.

When the girl left, James sank back in his chair, as if relaxing after a long day at work. It may have been my vacation, but it was his job.

"I can't believe this is the first time we're having dinner together," he said, staring at me with that puppy dog look of confusion.

It was a first date for two people who had been sleeping together for almost a week. The wine turned from maroon to crimson as it passed the candle flame on its way to our lips.

"I've never met anyone like you before," he said again. If I had not known better, I would have said he looked like a young boy falling in love. "Be careful, James," I said, as if it were he who needed protecting.

After dinner we walked back on the main street, the shops and restaurants now dark. We stopped in front of the brightly lit window of a real estate office, stopping to look at the photographs of houses for sale.

"How about this one?" James asked, pointing to a Mediterranean villa with a pool.

"No, too fancy," I replied, as if we were really shopping. "Look at this old farmhouse."

"It would need a lot of work."

We were standing under the yellow light, a spotlight in the center stage of the curved avenue. James leaned over and kissed me, twice. As if he were lost in the moment of a kiss on a first date, he did not look to see if anyone saw us.

The hotel was quiet when we returned. An old man sat hunched behind the main desk. He appeared to be dozing and I whispered when I asked for my key. It was as if a sleeping spell had been cast over our small castle. Maybe our first date ended with the kiss on the street, because we tiptoed up the curved marble staircase without any nervous anticipation. Time had become compressed in this make-believe place and

James and I had been together long enough for some things to become a familiar close to the day.

I do not remember falling asleep.

The brightness of morning felt like an invasion. The thin curtains were white flags blowing in the gentle breeze. I turned my head slowly to the left, surprised to see James's brown hair on the pillow next to mine. I had never allowed him to stay all night, to sleep beside me. I moved slowly across the sheets, inching my way to the edge of the bed. I was a soldier crawling on my belly through tall grass. He must have felt me move because then his face was next to mine, and I forgot what I was trying to escape. I would choose this beginning to my last day.

"So, you made it all the way through the night," I mumbled in a sleepy voice. I kissed him and whispered in his ear, "to the victor go the spoils." It can be the sweetest moment of the day.

At breakfast I sat with James. I was past pretending. "One last taste of lavender honey," I sighed, spreading it on my roll.

As we loaded the van I held back, making sure I sat in the front seat between Annie and James. I wore shorts and a sleeveless tee shirt because this was a beach day. Anticipating a beach day gave me a surge of excitement.

On Long Island, "going to the beach" meant The Ocean,

"People here quickly forget all their grief for the time being and then brim over with high spirits and illusions."

-Vincent van Gogh

the remarkable stretches of white sand along the Atlantic. As a very little girl, it meant holding my Daddy's hand as we ran away from the foamy end of an incoming wave. As a teenager I body surfed the waves, never tiring of the feeling of being propelled through the water. As a mother, trips to the ocean meant juice boxes in coolers and plastic pails and shovels and sharing my delight with my son. I keep a picture of him on my desk when he was eight years old, taken from the beach as he ran into the ocean. His arms are spread wide, ready to embrace it all. It is a photograph of the peak of anticipation. The image holds a promise that the ocean will deliver this moment again each summer.

I could smell the salty air as we drove through the vast marshlands of the Rhône delta. This was the Camargue, known for its herds of white horses, pink flamingoes and the *Gardiens* who work amongst the black bulls. The guidebook said, "these herders continue a two thousand year old tradition, making them the world's first cowboys."

As we drove through the endless grasslands, I looked out the window, hoping to catch a glimpse of white horses running free. The only white horses we saw were dirty, covered with brown dust, making them look more beige than white. They stood saddled, tethered in sad long lines by the side of the road, waiting for tourists. I imagined rescuing one from his degrading lot, the two of us disappearing through the tall grass in search of flamingoes and sandy beaches.

I was awakened from my daydream by the touch of James's fingers lightly making imaginary patterns on my bare leg. A newspaper was spread across my lap and he must have thought he was being very sneaky. Annie was driving and I stared straight ahead, but smiled.

The bright green marsh gave way to the seaside town of Saintes Maries de la Mer. A small tent city on the outskirts of town had been set up for the annual pilgrimage of the Gypsies. From all across Europe they gather here at the end of May for a five-hundred-year-old tradition that combines Christian legend, pagan festival and a little flamenco dancing. The town is named for the three Marys – Mary Magdalene, Mary Jacobe, Jesus's aunt, and Mary Salome, mother of apostles John and James.

The legend is that in 40 AD the three women and their servant Sarah were cast out to sea from Palestine in a boat without sails or oars, destined to meet a certain death. But they drifted across the Mediterranean and washed ashore there at the mouth of the Rhône River. In 1448 AD King René unearthed the "remains" of the Egyptian servant Sarah and Mary Salome, which are now kept in the crypt of the stone church in the center of town. During their festival, the Gypsies carry the statue of their saint, known as the Black Sarah, down to the sea, where the bishop, waiting in a fishing boat, bestows a blessing.

Unfortunately, we were a day too early for this ceremony, but just the idea of Gypsies sounded colorful and mysterious to me, like a Grimm's fairy tale. Others in the group were less intrigued.

"Where do you think we can find a bathroom?" Big John happened to ask.

"Maybe they have some in the Gypsy camp," I thought aloud.

"Yeah, well you can go there, if you don't want to come back," he snorted.

While Annie was locking the doors to the van, I heard her say to James, "You're not on your honeymoon, you know. Pay attention to the rest of the clients."

His covert move under the newspaper had not gone undetected by Annie. She sounded jealous, but not of me in particular. Clients. She needed to remind him of his responsibilities. Or maybe, she envied James having fun with a client while she was just working. Theirs was a world of brief encounters.

In the bright sunlight everything in Saintes Maries appeared white, set off by the primary colors outlining the tiny buildings, like a Mondrian painting. Streets fanned out from the town's center. It had the casual nonchalance of a beach town, except for the gray stone Romanesque church, Notre-Dame-de-la-Mer, standing alone on display as if anchoring the town square. We stood in the shadow cast by the church, a relief from the glare of the sun.

I followed the movement of people through the heavy wooden doors. I was caught in the flow as we moved right before entering the nave, then shuffling down stairs. The air was thick with the smell of religious candles and the dampness from the sea, and bodies moving forward as if entering the interior of a cave.

One end was aglow with burning candles. A priest stood in the yellow light speaking softly. The rhythm of his words penetrated the depth of the space, and I realized he was chanting. Mothers held small children by the hand, pushing them close to a primitive statue of a woman. Her face was painted pure black. I watched, like an intruder, as one mother placed her child's hand on the wooden folds of the Black Sarah's dress. As my eyes adjusted to the dark, I realized there were hundreds of candles burning in this crypt.

A line of crutches and canes leaned against the wall. Notes and pictures had been left at the foot of the statue. I stood in the darkness, not sure whether to move forward or go back. Finally, I climbed the stairs to the exit of Notre-Dame-de-la-

Mer. I had just witnessed a sacred ceremony.

"Did you go downstairs?" I said, looking at our group, standing like statues themselves in the shade of the church tower.

"No," Big John answered impatiently. "We're going down to the beach now."

I found my place in line as we marched the zigzag of narrow alleys, passing small shops selling colorful beachwear, toys and candies. The one-story wooden buildings looked like a miniature village made from children's blocks. When we emerged from this maze, a straight road led to the waterfront.

The harbor off to the right was filled with fishing boats, their masts covered with colorful triangular flags blowing in the wind. Two long jetties at either end reached toward each other like fingers from opposite hands, protecting and enclosing the harbor. In front of us was a curve of sandy beach. It beckoned to me. I took off my shoes and walked straight for the water. I felt the shock of cold on my feet, but kept wading deeper. The others remained clustered on the beach. It was still early in the day and the beach was mostly empty, so they appeared more like lost refugees than vacationers.

"How is it?" Charlie shouted.

"It's great," I said.

"Wait – I'll take your picture."

Annie followed him to the edge of the water. She waded toward me and Charlie coaxed us to pose. The wind blew her long brown hair and caught the scarf she wore loosely around her shoulders. It flowed behind her like the flags on the harbor's boats. She lowered her chin, smiling provocatively at the camera. I envied her natural beauty. She looked as if she had just emerged from the sea. As she would say, it was a moment of *sensualité.*

"I'm going to walk down the beach," I said to the huddled mass, but no one moved.

At the water's edge the cool sand was firm. I walked with my head down, looking for shells. I began to run, fast, following the curve where water met sand. I passed two women settled on blankets, keeping watch over small children digging near the tidal pools. I reached the jetty and climbed up onto the rocks. I stepped carefully, like a tightrope walker. Each rock was distinctive, this one small, that one big, most rough and jagged and slanted every which way.

I remembered climbing with my son on a jetty on the sandy beach near our home. He was very young, only three years old, and I had to cajole him. "Let's just make it to the big white one." Anyone on the beach would have thought I was being reckless with a small child. He could have slipped into the water. A big wave could have washed him off the rocks, but

I held his hand tightly. I wanted to share the excitement with someone.

I looked out to the end of the jetty as if it were the faraway summit of a mountain peak, then turned and made my way quickly back to the beach. When I reached the group I said, "Come on, somebody come and climb the jetty with me."

James and Charlie had gone back into town. The rest were content to sit in the sand, just wondering what was next on the itinerary. But Little John stood up and followed me down the beach to the jetty.

The first rocks at the edge of the tidal pools were slick with seaweed. My bare feet gripped the rocks, but John was slipping in his sneakers. At first we moved slowly across the uneven pile of stones. When he hesitated, staring bewildered at the jumble of rocks in front of him, I looked back and shouted, "Try that flat one over there."

Once I was sure he hadn't lost his balance, I began showing off, leaping from rock to rock. My arms were moving like wings, propelling me forward. The faster I moved, the more graceful I felt. I reached the last dry rock and looked down into the swirling sea. I stretched out my arms and yelled just to hear the wind take my voice.

Little John made it three quarters of the way down the jetty. When I turned to head back he was staring at me. "You looked like you were really having fun," he said.

"Yes, the rocks and the sea. They make me feel happy and just a little wild." He was silent, but I could see perplexity in his eyes. Odd woman, this climber of jetties.

Walking back together along the beach, John stayed on the dry sand while I followed the waterline, looking down as remains of small waves covered my toes.

"Did you see us on the rocks?" I asked James, who had returned and was sitting with the others on the sand. His arms were wrapped around his knees. "Yes, but you should have been wearing a diaphanous gown."

Looking down at my bare feet and baggy khaki shorts, I tried to picture myself in flowing silk, leaping across those rocks. I was not the diaphanous gown type, and besides I probably would have tripped on the fabric.

We left the beach for lunch, following the straight road lined with open-air restaurants. They were identical except for the color of their awnings, blue, red, green. At each entrance huge black pans overflowed with paella, mounds of yellow rice encrusted with pink shrimp, black mussels, clams and red lobster. It could have been the cover of any gourmet food magazine. Behind each display stood a man beaming, beckoning us to eat with him.

We settled at a place decorated with red tablecloths and

bullfighting posters on the back wall. Annie sat at the head of our table, her back to the street, watching over us. We ate our paella and drank cold beer. Charlie admired my Swiss Army watch and I bragged that I paid ten dollars for it in Chinatown. We took pictures of the table and the food and pictures of each other, laughing, chomping on shrimp, as if we were old, old friends traveling together.

I wanted to stay there all afternoon, to get drunk on the beer and forget about tomorrow. But our schedule intruded. Annie rose from the table, telling us to meet back at the church square in half an hour. Sue and Peg wanted to go shopping.

I wandered through side streets alone, looking in shop windows. All the stores were closed for lunch and the required siesta and I arrived at the square before anyone else. At a small outdoor café across the plaza, I ordered a coffee and sat at a table in the back, concealed by the shadows. As I took my first sip, looking over the top of the cup, I realized it was the perfect vantage point from which to watch our group congregate. I felt like a spy in some Cold War novel zeroing in on Sue and Peg as they appeared with Tim from behind the church. Their heads swiveled from side to side in search of familiar faces.

Little John walked over to them and they exchanged

"I have a lover's insight or a lover's blindness . . ."

-Vincent van Gogh

unheard greetings. It was like watching a silent movie. Across the square I saw Big John's head of gray hair above the crowd. He moved toward them with strong, deliberate steps. In his thigh-high shorts and hiking boots he looked more like a Norwegian Viking than an American tourist. Sue just looked hot and tired and sat on a bench. Little John glanced at his watch.

James moved into the scene now, walking quickly, his head jerking as he searched for his charges. Herding cats is what the guides call it. Hidden in my dark corner, watching their every move, I began to feel guilty. I paid for my coffee at the bar and strolled into the sunlight, the last stray cat. James looked up as I merged into the group.

"I was just having a coffee," I began to confess. He looked across the square.

"You were over there?"

Annie saved me and shouted over us, "Is everyone here? Let's go."

We marched in tired steps to our van. We drove out of town without ever seeing the Gypsy camp. My head rested on the back of the seat watching the green marsh grass flow to the horizon. The same row of horses, still tied together in lines, waited for their tourist cowboys to ride them to the sea.

"So, where are we headed now?" someone asked.

"Arles," Annie said. Arles. Another mandatory stop on the tourist circuit, noteworthy in the worlds of art, history and archaeology. It was to Arles that Van Gogh came in 1888, where he wandered with candles atop his straw hat at night along the Rhône River. It is where he painted another of his starry nights, and where he fought with Gauguin in the famous ear incident.

I wished I could have stood by the river and imagined that sky at night, or touched the walls of a narrow street and felt his rage and lonely hopelessness. Instead we parked outside the town wall and followed our leaders to the Roman amphitheater. Following can be the most efficient way to see the sights, but it surely does not encourage the adventure of discovery.

Obediently we admired the stone carving at the Cathédrale St. Trophine and climbed the stairs to the top of Les Arénes. I stood in a kind of time warp, using the gray stone arches built in the first century to frame my photographs of the town, with its orange tile roofs, geranium-filled window boxes and turquoise shutters. Turning and looking down into the amphitheater, I could almost see the gladiators and lions that once fought for their lives in the arena. Today their ghosts watch over the matadors and bulls in their dances with danger during the summer months.

As these incongruous images collided inside my head, we

walked back to the Place du Forum and planted ourselves under the yellow awning of Le Café la Nuit. With details worthy of Disney, the café had been meticulously maintained just as it was in Van Gogh's famous painting. Only the dark blue of the nighttime sky was missing at four in the afternoon. As American tourists, we knew how to behave in such places as this café whose image was on everything from tee shirts to coffee mugs. We drank glasses of Coca-Cola. Maybe we were just ready to go home.

James and Annie had left us, busy running errands in the town. Tomorrow they would begin a four-day break before meeting their new group. They were going to a small town in the hills of the Luberon. "That is my favorite place in all of Provence," Annie had said when she saw the road sign pointing the way to Sault. I overheard her tell James she had reserved rooms. "I am so happy. I was able to get room number five. She gave you number three."

James arrived first at the café and stood behind our row of chairs. "I was going to buy you a drink," he said to me, "but you already have one." Annie walked across the square waving to us. James straightened and called to her, "Did you find the lingerie shop?"

I turned my head sideways to Charlie and said over my shoulder, "They have a long weekend coming up."

"I was thinking the same thing," he said with a smile. I wondered if everyone in the group assumed they were lovers. When we first arrived in Saint Rémy, James and Annie had collected large envelopes from the post office. It was their outpost in southern France, where they received instructions from the home office and their personal correspondence. "Annie is all aglow," James had told me. "She got a letter from her boyfriend in Switzerland."

"Oh, I was wondering if the two of you ever . . ." I did not finish the question.

"No, no. She can be a tease, but she's one of the boys with us. After she read her letter from Didier she sighed and flipped her head back and said, "Ahh, ain't love grand?" He had said the last part trying to imitate a Southern accent, on top of his Australian one, stretching out the words. I had felt relieved, not so much for myself, but because I liked Annie.

In the café we were finishing our Cokes when Annie suddenly said, "Time to go. *Allez, les enfants!*" Retracing our steps, we followed the same street with the high wall out of the city. I ducked into a shop looking for a card to give James. It is customary to tip the guides at the end of a trip. I quickly chose one with a photo of a tall ship on the ocean. He had told me he liked sailing.

It occurred to me that actually I knew very little about

James. We had shared a moment of sweet simplicity within the complexities of real life. Like tasting the fresh rosé wine at the first picnic lunch, or my daring to swallow the gritty raw shellfish in the market, our moment was something to savor in memory. There was one night to come. It was not yet a memory.

Back at the hotel my comfortable room showed the signs of leaving. The lacy wallpaper was a dull backdrop to my overflowing suitcase and newly acquired parcels scattered across the chair. The cherubs on the ceiling were now just lifeless mounds of plaster.

James was sitting on the bed, his legs stretched in front of him, watching me pack. "We need a picture of us together," he said and grabbed my camera. I crouched behind him on the bed, my arms wrapped around his chest. He stretched out his arm in front of us and snapped the photo. The lens would capture only half of his face, so the picture would look like a lopsided Picasso portrait.

"Tell me what you are going to say to me at the train station tomorrow so I don't cry." I said.

"What if I say," he paused for effect, "I'm better at Hello?"

I laughed, before I realized he might be serious. Rolling back on the bed I said, "Yes, say that. It will make me laugh." But I could feel the stored up tears one silly line would not be able to stop. I did not want to think about tomorrow's early morning scene.

"At least you get to go to the Ritz," James said.

At a friend's suggestion, I had planned this one extravagance. After a hiking trip she told me, "You should have one night of luxury in Paris."

"You could join me," I said, continuing to pack.

"Ahh, the Ritz," he sighed, then watched me in silence for awhile.

When he spoke again he asked, "So, how are you in the garden?"

"Pretty good," I answered, as if it were a normal question. I remembered the vegetable garden I nurtured the summer I was pregnant.

"Do you play tennis?" he asked. His expression was serious, as if my answer was important.

"A little." I looked at him over the top of my glasses, coyly, smiling, not sure what this was all about.

"God," he laughed. "If you played tennis, I'd marry you." He said this to himself, as if I couldn't hear him.

"I guess you play."

"Yes. And I've never met a woman who could beat me."

I hated these games where there was always winner and loser. "I do have a mean cross court shot when I'm angry," I said.

"It would take more than that to beat the wild Aussie."

I looked at him over the top of my glasses and pointed my finger like a schoolteacher. "But remember, James, this time you've come across a Woman of Substance."

"Then what the hell are you doing with me?" He mumbled this into the air. I had already turned my back to him. It was as if we were speaking our own private soliloquies.

I had resumed packing and stopped to look out the window. "This song has been running through my head for the last couple of days," I said.

"Which one?" I heard him say.

"Hold on, my heart," I hummed, "Just hold on to that feeling. We both know we've been here before . . . We both know what can happen."

From the top of the stairs I could see our group waiting in the lobby for the drive to our last supper. I had finished my packing alone and dressed in my black pants and top, but tonight I tied a large maroon patterned scarf, folded in a triangle, around my waist. It fell off-center, a piece of Provence resting on my right hip. I was ready now for the pre-dawn departure the next day and for whatever the final night might hold.

The sun was low in the sky, its golden light casting long shadows across the landscape. Trees lined the road leaving

Saint Rémy and the stone houses became smaller. After half an hour of driving we pulled into a small churchyard and followed Annie across the road, through a white gate and down a flowered path to a small house. Window boxes overflowed with red geraniums. Next to a large freshly painted green door hung the sign Maison Trepanier. A short gray haired woman, Madame Trepanier herself, greeted us.

The restaurant was empty except for the early American diners. She showed us to a long narrow table set with china and crystal and flowers. James followed her toward the kitchen, gesturing in a familiar way. I chose a seat in the middle of the table, leaving my dinner partners to chance.

Charlie soon took his place beside me and Little John took the other side. When James returned he sat at the head of the table. He was wearing his blue jean shirt open at the neck, and I remembered it was the same shirt he had worn when we drank Pastis on the terrace in Sauveterre. He looked tan and relaxed and I almost had to stop myself from saying, "You know, honey, you really look great in that blue jean shirt." Instead, I palmed my small camera hoping to catch him unawares, but at the last second he turned and smiled right at the lens as if posing for *Gentleman's Quarterly.*

Our first course arrived – zucchini blossoms stuffed with salmon mousse. The yellow flowers seemed tiny bulging balloons, the green veins stretched taut across the delicate petals resembling a city road map. The engorged flowers were tied together at the end and the tips fanned out, hiding their smooth surprise. They floated in a sea of pale yellow cream flecked with herbs. It was more an ingenious creation than a delicious one and "James the chef" loved it. "Will you take a picture of this for me?" he asked.

Big John sat across the table from me. I took a bite and looked up at his face. His eyes were closed and his brow furrowed in concentration. His lips were taut, his jaw moved slowly as his tongue tasted his food. He was lost in the bliss of his private gourmet world. I nudged Charlie with my elbow. We watched big, burly John, a new convert to my prescribed method for sensuous dining.

At the end of our meal James went to the back of the restaurant to speak to the chef. He nuzzled close to me as I was returning from the ladies room. Eyeing my off-center scarf draped across my hip he said in a low voice, "My, you're looking very chic tonight, my dear."

When we left the restaurant the sky glowed like a sapphire, *gitane bleu* Annie called it, gypsy blue. A sliver of a white crescent moon hung low on the horizon. I sat between Annie and James in the front seat as we moved down the darkened roads. The conversation in the van was giddy, a cloud of laughter floating behind our heads. I drew my black shawl around my shoulders. It fell across my lap and onto James's leg.

The front seat of the van was dark, like a movie theater, as we watched the headlights illuminating the road. I let one hand creep under the soft fabric onto his leg as he drove. My hand followed the smooth worn trail of his jeans, playfully, but wistful also on the eve of departure.

At the hotel we scattered. Some of the others were hoping for a few hours of sleep before our early morning rendezvous. At the top of the stairs, James gave me a knowing nod and I turned in the direction of my room. In eight days we had gone from tentative flirts, to Hollywood style lovers, to here, where a nod was understood with the familiarity of an old married couple. I turned the key in my door, knowing he would appear shortly. After several minutes I heard his soft knock. He had a pile of papers in his hand.

"Take a look at the new trip I'm putting together," he said as he jumped onto the bed. It was his itinerary for Tasmania. "Can you get away in November?" he asked. "It's really beautiful there."

While I was looking at the papers, he pulled out an envelope of photographs.

"This is what I'll look like when I'm fifty," he said, showing me a picture of a gray haired man with a bushy mustache.

"That's my brother." He passed me photographs of his family. There was a picture of a young girl with dark brown bangs smiling in front of a fancy dessert in a glass goblet. "She came to visit me in Australia and I made her this dessert at the restaurant," James said, in the special way fathers talk about their daughters.

Later, in the dark, after we had made love he said, "I never got to take you camping." I wanted to stay awake all night. We lay side by side. He ran his hand down my arm. "Oh, Jenny," he whispered. The blue light from the street lamp cast a sad glow over the sheets, and I closed my eyes.

I heard the sharp beep of the alarm clock. My hand grabbed in the direction of the sound until I touched the small box and silenced it. It was still dark, a time between night and day, and I wasn't sure where I was. I rolled my head back onto the pillow, facing the ceiling. These movements took only seconds, an instinctive reaction done in semi-consciousness, and I would not have been surprised if I had gone back to sleep. But before I could be saved, two tears, on cue like synchronized swimmers, escaped from each corner of my closed eyes and traveled in straight lines downward into my hair.

James rolled over and kissed my wet cheek. "Ohhh," he

sighed. I felt betrayed by my body, caught unaware by these stealth tears. These were the tears that hid beneath the surface, complicated tears I kept subdued. These were not the acceptable tears that come at expected times of sadness or grief. I did not feel sad the way a young girl feels saying good-bye to her lover. I wasn't sure I felt sad at all. At least not for saying good-bye to James.

But I knew I would be saying good-bye to Jenny also. No matter how long a moment is we always want it to last longer, to hold on to it even when it is time to let it go. My moment had lasted eight days and still I was greedy. These tears were my punishment. And I knew these tears would put up a good fight to betray me before I could get on the train to Paris.

"I'd better go get ready," James said, and I nodded. Better to prepare for battle alone.

By the time I dragged my bag out the door of *chambre quatre*, the sun had brightened the sky. It made me feel somewhat justified wearing sunglasses.

The town was still asleep. There was no happy chatter from our groggy group, only the sound of gravel crunching under our feet as we walked across the courtyard and into the van. I sat far in the back by the window. James drove while making small talk with Annie and the others. I bit my lower lip hard and clenched my fists, digging my fingernails into the palms of my hands. Look up at the treetops, I told myself, see the sun just starting to turn the leaves into opaque green stained glass. Where are the poppies, find the poppies. My fingernails left painful indentations in the soft padding of my palms.

When we reached Avignon my eyes were dry, and I walked with determination into the station. We stood clumped in a circle around our bags while Annie and James went to get our tickets. At seven in the morning the neon sign of Le Snak Bar might as well have said, "Go Away." A woman in uniform was mopping the floor of the station with gray water. I heard bits and pieces of the small talk surrounding me. "Where are you going next? . . . home? . . . Just think, tonight you'll be having dinner in Paris."

Annie passed out the tickets. "You are in different cars. You're all in the first car, except Jennifer, Tim and Peg. You are in car number twelve." James carried my bag as we crossed under the tunnel and up the stairs to the platform. As a group we shook hands, said our embarrassed good-byes, knowing we would not see each other again, wanting this part to be over quickly.

"I'll stay with them at this end of the platform," Annie was saying. "You take the others to the front."

I was biting my lip again. I pretended it was my hair I was

brushing from my cheek, and not the tear that had escaped from behind my sunglasses. I looked at James and for a moment we both smiled a feeble, helpless smile. I did not watch as he turned and led the group away.

The colors of Provence felt as if they had been washed from me with one splash from the cleaning woman's bucket. Surrounded by the grays of the train station, I headed to my end of the platform. Tim peered down the tracks for the train and Peg asked Annie how she would spend the rest of the day.

At the far end of the station, the others had become small anonymous dots. I turned and faced Annie, willing myself not to look toward the far end again. There was compassion in Annie's eyes, as if she wanted to reach out and hold me, like a sister. She had experience with these train station good-byes. Maybe she knew the best way to do it, but I felt something close to panic as the minutes passed. This was not the way it should end.

Someone was running, out of breath. "Why don't we switch places?" James asked, as his face appeared from behind Annie. She smiled her big smile, tossed her hair and waved as she walked away. I heard the train whistle and instinctively reached for the handle of my suitcase.

"I couldn't let you leave without saying good-bye," James said, as he touched my hand.

The train stopped in front of us and he helped carry all the bags on board. I stood aside, letting Tim and Peg enter the seating compartment, and followed James back onto the platform. We kissed with our arms wrapped around each other, a kiss as strong as the first, one to remember. And then I turned and climbed back on the train. I did not look back. I never look back after good-bye. I try to walk in that time tunnel between then and now without slipping. I always try to be brave.

I chose a seat in the middle of the almost empty car, away from Tim and Peg. Through the grimy window I saw James, his head moving side to side, looking into the train. I stood up, fumbling in my purse as if I had forgotten something.

As I made my way to the rear of the car, I pretended to check the baggage, then climbed back down several steps toward the platform. I stood on the last step while James reached up to me. Clinging to each other we kissed again and again. My cheeks were wet with unselfconscious tears. The train heaved in warning before the wheels began to turn.

James waved and I saw his lips move.

"Good-bye, Jenny."

MICHAEL FAIRCHILD

"How rich art is; if one can only remember what one has seen, one is never without food for thought or truly lonely, never alone."

-Vincent van Gogh

ARTHUR LAWRENCE

Jennifer Huntley has been a radio news reporter, actor, tour guide, mother, traveler, and freelance writer. This travel memoir is her first book. She lives in New York City and Long Island.